BERNIE JONES
AND THE
BLAZING BANDITS

Sharon Bushell

Sharon Bushell

For Ms. M's class
with best wishes!

Keep Reading!

SHARON BUSHELL

BERNIE JONES AND THE BLAZING BANDITS

ILLUSTRATED BY KATIE MILLER

ROAD TUNES MEDIA
HOMER, ALASKA
2005

ROAD TUNES MEDIA
534 Hidden Way
Homer, Alaska 99603
roadtunes@gci.net

Cover Art Work by Katie Miller and W.B. Hughes
Cover Design/Layout by Road Tunes Media
Manufactured in the United States of America

October 2005   First Edition

10 9 8 7 6 5 4 3 2 1
Library of Congress Cataloging-in-Publication Data
Bushell, Sharon   Bernie Jones and the Blazing Bandits
Summary: Bernie finds himself involved in more humorous and learning adventures in the 1950s.
1. Children's stories. (1. Friends- Fiction. 2. Pets-Fiction 3. 1950s - Fiction. 4. Growing Up - Fiction)
I. Title. p. 144   26 b/w drawings. Illustrated by Miller, Katie

ISBN-13: 978-0-9721725-5-4
ISBN-10: 0-9721725-5-6
Library of Congress Control Number: 2005907728

http://www.berniejones.com

With love for Josh and Jon

CONTENTS

There's a Mouse in the House!

All his life, Bernie Jones was fascinated by the great outdoors and the many creatures that occupy it. Along with bugs and worms and snakes, he had a particular fondness for mice. Recently, after a class field trip to the pet shop, his desire to have a small white mouse for his very own grew so strong that he attempted what he knew was a hopeless venture: convincing his mother that such a pleasant little creature would be a treat for the entire family.

When Bernie politely asked for permission to buy and care for one small, extremely tidy white mouse, Mrs. Jones just as politely said no, and from that position she did not budge. Determined to get his way, Bernie broke the promise he made to himself and began to beg and plead, though he knew it was a waste of time. To reinstate his dignity, he switched to a different tactic: making well-intended promises - to study more, to antagonize his sister Charmaine less, to remember to feed his dog Weezer, to do all his chores without having to be nagged. He made so many promises, he couldn't remember them all without a list, which, unfortunately, he quickly lost.

Figuring he had nothing to lose, he was at this moment making one last attempt to persuade his mother.

"Absolutely not," said Mrs. Jones. "We already have two children, a dog and a cat. The last thing we need is another pet." What she didn't say, because everyone in the family already knew, was that she was terrified of mice.

Coincidentally, next door at Brian Shaunessey's house, another conversation about mice was taking place. The Shaunessey family was leaving for a two-week vacation - they were just getting ready to walk out the door - when Brian suddenly remembered that he hadn't found anyone to watch his three pet mice. His teacher, Mrs. Zimmer, had said they could stay in her classroom during the week, but he'd have to make other arrangements for the weekends. His parents were now in such a panic, Mrs. Shaunessey could barely speak.

With so many things on her mind, she was in no mood for last-minute problems. The taxi was already on its way, for goodness sake! Through tightly clenched teeth she said, "If you don't find someone in the next five minutes to take care of those mice, you'll just have to turn them loose in the yard and let them take care of themselves!"

"We can't turn them loose in the yard!" Brian whimpered. "I'll never find them again!" He grabbed the wire cage containing the three white mice and hurried out the door.

Wouldn't you know it ... the first person he saw was good old Bernie Jones. Brian began running toward him and speaking so fast, Bernie could barely understand what he was saying.

"Bern! You're just the guy I was looking for. I need to ask you a big favor. My parents are about to go ballistic on account of that we have to leave for the airport in a couple minutes and I forgot to find someone to take care of my mice. Mrs. Zimmer says they can stay in her classroom on school days, so it's only for the weekends. If I don't find someone to watch them in the next five minutes, my mom says I have to turn them loose in our yard."

Brian took a deep breath, wiped a layer of sweat from his brow, and continued, "Their whole lives, they've never been anywhere except their cage. They don't even know there *is* anywhere else. The yard is a nice place for humans, but for a mouse, it's a jungle! They'll get lost! A cat will get them! They'll die out there, Bern! If you have an ounce of compassion ... please, you've gotta help me."

Bernie wasn't exactly sure what compassion was, but he figured he probably had at least an ounce of it. He was also pleased that Brian had come to him with his problem; in the old days, that never would have happened.

As Brian made his plea, Bernie considered his new, upgraded status in the neighborhood: though they were both ten years old, he and Alex were now official members of the Blazing Bandits. After all these years, they finally got to tag along with the big boys and be part of whatever activity they were involved in. Their initiation - each boy had to eat a quart of mayonnaise - had been as difficult for Alex as it was easy for Bernie. In fact, Alex could only force down a few bites before having to run to the bushes, where the white gooey stuff promptly came back up.

Fourteen-year-old Clark Olsen, the president of the club, decided the two boys could still pass the initiation if Bernie were able to eat both jars. To the shock and thrill of everyone concerned, Bernie completed the task in record time. Though they were two years younger than any of the other Blazing Bandits, they were finally included in all the activities and fun. For Bernie and Alex, it was a dream come true.

The initiation had taken place months ago, but Bernie would still do pretty much anything to stay in good with a brother Bandit, especially if it concerned the well-being of three mice. The thought of the poor little creatures struggling for survival in the jungle of the Shaunessey's neatly tended yard made Bernie shudder. He peered into the wire cage, which Brian took as a positive response.

"This is Snowball." Brian reached into the cage. "You can tell

because he's so skinny. No matter how much I feed him, he never seems to get any bigger." He placed the furry little mouse in Bernie's hands and continued his explanation. "But Winnie and Miss Josephine, they just keep getting fatter and fatter. I don't understand it. They must be hogging all the food."

Just then the taxicab pulled into the Shaunessey's driveway. "You saved me, Bern. Thanks a lot. You're really a pal." Brian thumped Bernie on the back, told him a few more details about the care of the mice, then ran toward his family and the waiting cab.

Everything had happened so fast, Bernie felt like his head was spinning. Ten minutes ago he was pleading with his mother for one mouse; now he had three. Had he really agreed to watch them? It would undoubtedly lead to trouble. But what could he do? Brian was gone. He had the mice. He had to take care of them.

He glanced over his shoulder, scanning his driveway and yard for any movement. Somehow, without letting anyone in his family know about it, he had to smuggle the mice into the house and find a place to hide them.

The basement had always been Bernie's favorite room, so that's where he went, cage in hand. He chose a spot next to the laundry table, by the washer and dryer. It was warm there, plus it was nice and dark. He was sure that Snowball and Winnie and Miss Josephine would like it. He carefully settled the cage in its hiding spot, then ran upstairs to the kitchen to grab a handful of Cheerios and some lettuce leaves. He knelt down in front of the cage and let the scraps of food fall from his hand. "Here you go, guys. I hope you like it here. I'll be back a little bit later. Try not to make any noise."

It turned out that hiding the mice was easy; the hard part was staying out of the basement. Now that he had three mice to take care of, all Bernie wanted to do was hang around and watch them.

Dreamer, the Jones's big calico cat, was the only creature in the house that Bernie had not fooled. The minute he appeared with the cage in his hand, Dreamer awoke from her nap with the knowledge that something new was in the house. Something that smelled delicious. She saw Bernie sneak downstairs to the basement. She considered following him, but decided she would find out what was going on in her own good time. For now, she preferred laying in the sunshine, licking her paws, slowly falling asleep to the thought of her beauty and intelligence.

Later on, when she caught another tantalizing whiff of rodent, Dreamer snuck down the stairs to have a look around. She had no trouble finding the cage. One ... two ... three, she counted the mice, planning which she would eat first. Of course there was the problem of the cage, but when the time was right, she wouldn't let a thing like that stop her.

✱✱✱✱✱✱✱✱✱

Without arousing the suspicion of anyone in the family, Bernie managed to visit the basement four times the first day. Each time he lingered just a little longer, it was such fun to watch the mice. Not that they did much. Mostly they just sat there, twitching their noses or burrowing in their straw. Bernie wanted to hold each of them, but seeing as how Winnie and Miss Josephine were best friends and didn't seem to want any other company, Snowball was the only one Bernie picked up.

Bernie was starting to get so attached to the mice, he was sorry that he had to take them to school on Monday and leave them with Mrs. Zimmer. All too soon his mouse adventure would be over, and life would go back to normal.

But that's not the way it turned out.

The next morning, when Bernie crept down to the basement to say good morning to Snowball and Winnie and Miss Josephine, he saw something that made his mouth drop open in amazement. There in the cage, along with the three grownup mice, were at least a dozen babies. They were so tiny, at first Bernie couldn't even figure out what they were. Each of them was about the size of his fingertip and totally pink, with not one bit of fur.

Two feelings hit Bernie at the same time. All of these teeny tiny baby mice had been born in his house. A big smile spread across his face. He felt like a brand new uncle.

His next thought was not so happy. "Oh brother," he said out loud, imagining what the family would do when they found out.

Mrs. Zimmer was his only hope. On Monday Bernie got to school early and went straight to her classroom. He took a deep breath to bolster his courage and said, "I was supposed to bring Brian's mice to your class today."

"Mmmm hmmm." Mrs. Zimmer didn't even look up. She was sitting at her desk, correcting papers.

"But I think you should know that just last night both Winnie and Miss Josephine had ... babies. Lots of babies."

"What's that you say?" said Mrs. Zimmer, glancing up, her glasses dangling perilously close to the edge of her nose. "Babies? Mouse babies?" She stood up, gathered a bundle of papers, then turned to face Bernie. "I'm afraid this changes everything. I told Brian that while he was on vacation he could bring three mice into my classroom, but certainly not a lot of baby mice! No! No! Heavens no! I couldn't possibly allow it." She walked out the door and down the hall.

Oh brother, thought Bernie, what am I gonna do now? I can't keep the mice in the basement for two whole weeks. *Anything can happen in two weeks.* He imagined Charmaine finding the mice and going into a screaming fit, the neighbors calling the police, the fire department barging in, the Jones's house destroyed in the process.

I know what to do, Bernie decided. I'll go see Grandpa. He always gives me good advice.

The minute school was over, Bernie hurried down to the senior center and went straight to the room of Augustus Jones. As usual, Grandpa was sitting in his easy chair playing cribbage with his old friend, Fred Jenkins.

"Howdy Dowdy!" he said, spotting Bernie in the doorway. "Come on in. You can watch your grandpa beat this poor old feller here for the third time today. Last time I skunked 'im, too."

"No one likes a braggart, Augustus," Mr. Jenkins mumbled.

Bernie was almost out of breath. "I've got a big problem I have to take care of, Grandpa." He explained all about his predicament.

Grandpa was completely absorbed in his cribbage game and didn't offer the kind of help Bernie was hoping for. "Yep, that's a dandy of a problem," Grandpa said. "Yessirree Bob. Your mother catches you with mice in the house, you're gonna have a whole lot of trouble. My advice is ... good luck!"

"But Grandpa, you haven't told me what to do."

"Sorry, bud. Some problems you have to figure out all on your own. It's good practice."

"But ... but ..."

Grandpa reached to pick up the cards Mr. Jenkins had dealt him. Bernie left the room. "Let me know how it all works out!" Grandpa shouted. "I surely will be interested to hear!"

When Bernie arrived home he headed straight for the basement to check on the mice. At first everything looked okay. All the babies were laying next to their mothers, peacefully drinking milk.

Snowball's behavior was strange, though. He hovered in the corner, looking disturbed, his tiny brown eyes darting from Josephine to Winnie and back again. He hadn't touched his food, and he had a worried look about him. Even though Bernie had just read it in a school library book, he had a hard time believing that Snowball might try to hurt the babies. He thought about it for quite a while, then he got up and, figuring it was better to be safe than sorry, began searching for another box.

The best he could come up with was a big cardboard box with tall sides and open on the top. Bernie tore up some newspapers, found an old soft cloth for Snowball to sleep on, then transferred him to his new home. "You'll like it here, boy," he said. "It's nice and quiet, and here's a little rug for you to curl up on. Those baby mice won't give you any trouble at all in here."

✳✳✳✳✳✳✳✳✳

One by one the days passed. No one in Bernie's family seemed to think it unusual that he spent so much time in the basement. Not only did he have to bring the mice water and food each day, he felt it was important to spend time with Snowball, to make up for the fact that he was living all alone. Bernie had built him a cabin of Lincoln Logs and pasted a variety of pictures on the walls of the cardboard box.

By now Bernie had been able to get an accurate count of the baby mice. Fourteen! Both Winnie and Miss Josephine each had seven children and all of them looked exactly alike. "I sure am going to hate to give you guys up," he said to all seventeen mice, but especially to Snowball. "We've got a regular family going on down here."

Meanwhile, Dreamer had been waiting patiently for her opportunity to get at the mice. She had considered the problem of the wire cage over and over, and so far she hadn't been able to figure out what to do. Now, however, crouching on the basement stairs, she saw something new. Where there used to be just one cage, there were two, and the new one would be easy to get into. *Most interesting*, she purred. Creeping back up the stairs, she began putting together a plan for a fine mousey meal with which to end the day.

As Bernie lay in bed that night, the fact that he was hiding seventeen mice in the house started to bother him again. During the day there was too much to do to think about it, but at night it always worked its way into his mind, making it hard to go to sleep. Looking back on it, it seemed as if he hadn't really had any choice in the matter, Brian had been so desperate. Still, Bernie knew that if his mother discovered seventeen mice in the basement, she would flip out. She hated mice almost as much as she hated snakes.

Bernie could not imagine feeling the way she did, for he had always loved the creeping, crawling, slithering, furry things of the world. In the darkness of his bedroom, he sighed and thought to himself, *as much as I don't want to give the mice up, I sure wish Brian would hurry and get home.*

✳✳✳✳✳✳✳✳✳

It was after midnight now. Dreamer stood at the top of the stairs, carefully licking each of her paws. *No sense being in too much of a hurry about this mouse business,* she told herself. *A cat must groom herself to perfection before a hunt.* When her multicolored fur was fully licked and gleaming, when her paws were thoroughly cleaned, she swiped the right one several times over the top of her head. At last she was ready. Silently she started down the stairs.

Snowball was having a late-night snack in the privacy of his box. He gnawed on a lettuce leaf, trying to decide what to have next. He missed the company of Winnie and Miss Josephine, but all the little creatures made him so nervous that, even though he was often lonely, he preferred the peace and quiet of his new home. Another benefit to this place was that it was made of cardboard, which Snowball had discovered he could easily chew through. He had already started on his escape route. So far he'd only accomplished a tiny hole, but through it he had glimpsed the big, dark room with its many hiding places.

Frequently, in the home of the boy named Brian, Snowball had escaped the confines of his cage and discovered that the world was HUGE! The world, in fact, was much bigger than just the boy's bedroom. It contained many rooms, full of all kinds of delightful things. Each time he escaped, after a day or two of freedom, Snowball would allow himself to be captured, for the pure and simple joy of coming back to his two best friends and dazzling them with his tales of adventure.

In this new home, in just a few days, his hole would be big enough that he could come and go whenever he pleased. He could visit Winnie and Miss Josephine. He could explore the big dark room. He would study the comings and goings of the family. He chomped into the crunchy goodness of a Cheerio and considered himself one very lucky mouse.

In the next moment, everything changed. Snowball was suddenly aware of the presence of an enemy. Because he had lived his entire life in the room of the boy called Brian, and since that family had no cat, Snowball had no knowledge of these great furry beasts. Nevertheless, all alone in his box, he knew

23

instinctively that an enemy was lurking. His tiny mouse heart began thumping so hard, he dropped his Cheerio and scurried for cover into the Lincoln Log house.

Crouching low in front of Snowball's box, Dreamer jumped easily inside. She couldn't see the mouse at first, but a quick look around revealed his hiding place. Snowball was so distressed when he saw the orange, white and black monster, all he could do was hide his face in the corner of the log house and squeak. "Please don't eat me! Please please please don't eat me!"

Dreamer, who did not understand mouse talk, opened her jaws and closed them on the small white mouse. An expert hunter, she knew exactly how much pressure was needed to keep the squirming thing from getting away without harming so much as a single strand of its fur. The Cat Code of Conduct, unofficial but known to cats the world over, has strict procedures in regard to feasting on a mouse.

As easily as she had pounced into the cardboard box, Dreamer now leaped back out, her jaws carefully cradling the panicked mouse. Not only did she intend to play with it a bit before eating it, it was important that she present it to her favorite person, the one who fed her each and every day: Mrs. Jones.

As Dreamer daintily walked up the stairs, Snowball, who was smarter than most mice, considered what a tragedy it was that his young life was about to end. He told himself he shouldn't have been so lazy. All the time he spent snacking and lazing about, he should have worked harder chewing through the box. If he had, he wouldn't be trapped inside the mouth of a quick and clever giant. Now it was too late for his plans and dreams of escape, of journeying into the big room, of exploring all the many things there were to explore. With all his might, Snowball wished he were back in the room of the boy called Brian and that none of this had ever happened.

Dreamer took her time, savoring each moment as she made the journey up the stairs toward the bedroom of Mr. and Mrs. Jones. They were both sound asleep when Dreamer entered their room.

What a nice surprise this will be, thought the cat as she jumped onto the bed. She crept to the space between the two sleeping people and waited for them to awaken. After only a few meows (which is difficult with a mouse in your mouth), Mrs. Jones woke up. Then everything went crazy.

When Mrs. Jones saw the white mouse wedged in Dreamer's mouth, she screamed and jumped out of bed. Mr. Jones, groggy and half asleep, struggled from the bed and, in his haste, pulled the bedspread along with him. This caused Dreamer to lose her balance, roll over and drop the mouse, who scurried to the edge of the bed and took a magnificent leap.

Never before had little Snowball done anything so brave as jumping off the Jones's bed. He couldn't see what there was to land on, and at that moment he didn't care. Getting away from the multicolored monster was his only concern.

On the rug, Snowball scampered toward the first thing he saw to hide behind, Mrs. Jones's feet. "Oh no!" she shrieked, "he's going to bite me! Quick, Michael, grab one of your golf clubs!" She shifted her weight from one foot to the other, doing a little dance, hopping back and forth, all the while screaming

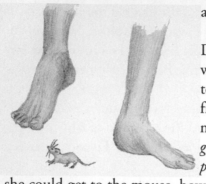

as loud as she could.

Dreamer was so upset by the way the people were reacting to her gift, she jumped down from the bed to retrieve the mouse. *If this is the way they're going to be, I'll just take my prize somewhere else.* Before she could get to the mouse, however, a paperback book came zinging through the air, missing her by mere inches. Also, the big human had something in his hand, which he was swinging as he hollered, "Go on! Get out! Bad cat!" Mr. Jones wasn't actually going to hit Dreamer, but he wanted her to think he might.

Mrs. Jones continued hopping up and down, while Snowball did his best to hide from the cat. All of this took place in just a few minutes, but it seemed like forever to all concerned. When Bernie and Charmaine heard all the screaming, they came running to the bedroom, which added another element of chaos to the scene.

"Dad! No! Don't hit Snowball!" Bernie shouted.

Mr. Jones had no plan to harm the mouse; without his glasses he could barely even see it. Bernie knelt down and picked up Snowball. "Poor guy. You poor little guy," he whispered. "You must be scared to death." He nuzzled the fur on the top of Snowball's head.

Mrs. Jones stopped hopping long enough to scold her son. "Bernie! I can't believe you're holding that awful thing. Get it away from your face. Ick! It might bite you."

"He won't hurt me ... He's my friend ... His name is Snowball ..." Bernie started each sentence without knowing what he could possibly say to finish it. "I was only supposed to watch them for two days ..."

"*Them?*" said his mother. "Do you mean to tell me ... there is *another* mouse in this house?"

Bernie gulped and said, "Well it's really not as bad as it sounds but actually there are *seventeen* mice in the house."

Saying it out loud, it really did seem pretty bad.

Snowball's tail swished against Mrs. Jones's toes, causing an enormous shudder to run the length of her body. She started her little dance all over again. The screaming, too.

Mr. Jones was wide awake now. He stared, open-mouthed, at his son, amazed that his own flesh and blood could have done something so foolish. "Come on, Bernie," he said, motioning toward the door. "Let's get that mouse back in its cage right away. I assume there *is* a cage?"

Bernie was relieved that he had the right answer. "Yes, there's a cage. And a box, too. Downstairs in the basement." He was glad for a reason to get away from his mother.

After they left, Charmaine turned to her mother and wasted no time telling her what to do. "If you ask me, I think Bernie should be grounded for the rest of his life." She folded her arms high across her chest. "Plus no more birthdays or Christmases." Nothing made Charmaine quite so happy as seeing her brother punished.

When Bernie and his father got to the basement, Winnie and Miss Josephine were peacefully feeding their children. "Well what'dya know," Mr. Jones said when he saw all the baby mice. "Look how tiny these little guys are." He squatted down to take a long look and soon a big grin spread across his face. He went to stand at the bottom of the stairs and shouted, "Charmaine! Come on down here. I want you to take a look at this. Margaret, you ought to come, too."

Charmaine scurried toward her father's voice, and when Mrs. Jones calmed down, she followed her family to the basement. After all, sixteen mice inside a cage is a whole different thing than being awakened by one in your bed. With everyone gathered around the cage and the mouse babies feeding, even Mrs. Jones had to admit they were awfully cute.

After a while Mr. Jones herded the children back up the stairs to their bedrooms. "Let's all try to get some sleep now," he said. "We've had enough excitement for one night. First thing tomorrow, Bernie, we've got to find a better box for Snowball. Something a whole lot sturdier than cardboard."

As soon as the humans left him alone in the basement, little Snowball went into a frenzy of activity. Never had he chewed so furiously or frantically. He couldn't get the picture of the big cat out of his mind. And that screaming human who kept hopping around ... she was almost worse! It had been the most frightening experience of his young life. Chomp chomp chomp chomp chomp chomp went his tiny jaws, his strong front teeth gnawing at the cardboard. He was getting closer,

closer.

A few more chomps and he was free. He made a mad dash for the washing machine. Once he was behind it, he felt the delightful feeling of safety wash over him. Staring out at the big room, his curiosity cheered him enormously. He had so much exploring to do, and he was certain he'd find plenty of food to eat. When the huge orange and black and white beast came looking for him again, he'd have a thousand places to hide.

As Bernie lay in his bed, he couldn't help thinking how amazing it was that everything had worked out so well. His secret was out in the open. There was nothing more to hide. He could relax and enjoy his time with the mice. He breathed a huge sigh of relief and drifted toward sleep.

He had no idea that Snowball had just escaped. Or that in the morning, when his mother went downstairs to do a load of laundry, she would again be surprised by the sudden appearance of the small white mouse, scurrying across the basement floor. As the family slept in innocent bliss, none of them realized that, as of now, Snowball had taken up permanent residence in their home.

In the last few moments before he fell asleep, Bernie made a promise to himself. "Now that I am out of this predicament, I will never *ever* get in trouble again."

Maryann Loves Bernie

Maryann Hastings stared at the back of Bernie Jones's head and tried to decide which mean thing to say to him. She had a large selection of things from which to choose. She could insult his dog, ridicule his sloppy handwriting, tease him about his unruly hair; the list went on and on. She had been pestering him this way all year, actually, ever since kindergarten, when he accidentally spilled a jar of paint in her hair.

But just as Maryann prepared to jab the eraser end of her pencil into Bernie's shoulder and whisper an insult in his ear, something happened. Something totally shocking. Maryann completely lost the impulse to be mean or to tease Bernie in any way. In fact, what she felt like doing was ... being nice to him.

This surprised her so much, she sat upright in her desk, crossed and uncrossed her eyes several times and shook her head a little, to get herself thinking straight again. She focused on the wisps of his hair that stuck out at odd angles, on the smudges of dirt on his neck. There was so much to make fun of, but the desire was totally gone. She put her pencil into her backpack and slumped down in her desk. She had never felt like this before.

Since kindergarten, Maryann and Bernie had always been in the same class. This year, at the first opportunity, Bernie had moved to a desk all the way across the room, as far away from Maryann as he could get. But within a few days, thanks to Chuckie Wadsworth and some of the other troublemakers, the entire seating assignment had to be rearranged, and Maryann moved in behind Bernie.

Actually, that worked well for Maryann. Some boys you could be mean to - accidentally thump them with your books or kick the back of their chair - and they might turn around and shove all your papers onto the floor, or snap your pencil in two. But Bernie, no matter how much she tormented him, just sat there and took it. Oh sure, he would snarl up his face and roll his eyes and sigh loud frustrated sighs, but he never told on her or tried to get her in trouble in any way.

Leaning heavily on her chin, doodling mindlessly on her paper, Maryann thought about all the mean things she had done and said to Bernie over the years, and how he never once did any mean thing, even when he had the chance. Then, like a light bulb turning on, it occurred to her that Bernie Jones was a genuinely nice person. He was probably the nicest person in the whole class. Maybe even the whole school. At that moment, although she was not aware of it, Maryann's scribbling

31

turned from random squiggles into a beautifully bordered heart. Twenty minutes later, when she completed it, right in the center of the heart, in her very best handwriting, she wrote, "Maryann plus Bernie equals love."

Bernie was reviewing his history lesson, watching the teacher write the day's assignments on the board and trying to remember if he had closed the gate when he left the house this morning. Lately he had fallen into the habit of not remembering to close it, which allowed Weezer to escape and then roam around town. That was fine with Weezer, but not fine with Mrs. Jones, who occasionally had to fetch him from the dog pound. If Bernie had left the gate open he could definitely expect to be in trouble when he got home. He sighed and stared off into space. Suddenly it occurred to him ... Maryann hadn't poked him in the shoulder all morning, and instead of saying anything mean, all she had said was, "Good morning, Bernie."

Her behavior was so unusual, after a while Bernie started wondering if there might be something wrong with her. He had known her for so long; he could tell when she was off track.

The fact that all she had said so far was "good morning," wasn't a Maryann kind of thing at all. If she had told him his feet were too big, or that he had the ugliest dog in the world, that would be much more like her. But, "good morning"? Maybe she was planning to trick him in some way. She had done that many times before. He decided he'd better be on his guard. Not only was Maryann acting weird; Mrs. Broadbottom was the substitute teacher today, and whenever she was around, Bernie was likely to get into trouble.

When the bell rang for recess, Maryann, instead of racing to the front of the class and rummaging through the big cardboard box of playground equipment for the best jump rope, got a basketball instead. When Bernie walked past her in the hall, she tried to hand it to him. This startled Bernie so much, he thought maybe she had somehow managed to get to the equipment box in time to smear the basketball with glue, or jam. He gave her a look like she was crazy. No way was he going to touch it. He just kept right on walking.

Instead of playing basketball, which really was his first choice, Bernie played four square. He couldn't keep his mind on his game, though. Whenever he glanced up, he could tell, even though Maryann was halfway across the playground jumping rope with her girlfriends, she was watching him.

After recess she did an even more puzzling thing. While the other kids were hanging up their coats and taking off their boots, she snuck into her lunch sack, removed the chocolate cupcake her mother had packed for her and put it on the corner of Bernie's desk.

She had such an unusual smile on her face when she set it

down, Bernie knew she must be planning something evil. And sure enough, before he had time to give the cupcake back to her, there was Mrs. Broadbottom clomping down the aisle.

"And just what is *this*?" she asked, snatching it from his desk and holding it up for all the class to see.

Bernie squirmed in his chair. His face turned bright red. "Um, it's a chocolate cupcake."

"I can *see* that," said Mrs. Broadbottom. "What I want to know is, what is it doing on your desk? It is not lunch time, young man."

"I don't know what it's doing on my desk," Bernie answered honestly.

"Well perhaps if you spent some time out in the hall you would remember," said Mrs. Broadbottom, pointing toward the door.

"Yes, Ma'am," Bernie said.

Maryann slumped down in her chair and tried to become invisible. She hadn't meant to get Bernie in trouble. She considered raising her hand and admitting it was really her cupcake, but Mrs. Broadbottom was one of those unpredictable kind of people who, if you told them the truth about things, sometimes you got rewarded and sometimes you got punished.

Bernie stood all alone in the hall, kicking the toe of his tennis shoe against the wall, frowning. *That darn old Maryann! Why would she want to get him in trouble? Now he would probably have to stay after school and clean the blackboards. It was Friday! He and Alex had planned to put up the Davy Crockett tent and go camping in the backyard.*

Sure enough, when the last bell rang, Mrs. Broadbottom announced, "Everyone is excused, except for Bernie Jones." Then she motioned toward the blackboards and to the big stack of dirty erasers.

By the time he finally got home, Bernie was sneezing from all the chalk dust. Alex already had the tent set up and, sitting on the front porch, laughing with Charmaine, was Maryann Hastings. "Hello, Bernie," she said. "I'm working on a report with your sister. Did you know that we're in the same Girl Scout troop?"

Charmaine knew how Bernie felt about Maryann. She snickered into her hand, pretending to cough.

Bernie breezed into the house, ran upstairs, grabbed his sleeping bag and hurried out the back door. "Don't worry about me for dinner," he told his mom. "Alex and I are going to roast hotdogs."

"All right dear!" she said, blowing him a kiss. In the next instant he was gone.

"Too bad you got sent to the hall today," said Alex, as he and Bernie were gathering wood for their campfire. "While you were out there, Judy McFadden accidentally knocked over a box of art supplies. It landed on Chuckie's science experiment. You know, all those little boxes full of dead beetles. Mrs. Broadbottom got really mad at her." Behind his thick glasses,

Alex's eyes seemed several times larger than they really were. "By the way, Bern, why the heck *did* you put that cupcake on your desk?"

"I didn't," said Bernie. "Maryann put it there."

"*Maryann Hastings?*" said Alex, gesturing toward the Jones's house. Bernie nodded yes.

"Why would she give *you* her cupcake?"

Bernie held up his palms. "I don't know. I've been trying to figure it out all day. Maybe she poisoned it."

Alex stared at the setting sun, seriously considered Bernie's idea for a moment, then said, "Yeah, you might be right."

✳✳✳✳✳✳✳✳✳

Upstairs in Charmaine's bedroom, the two girls lay on the floor with encyclopedias scattered all around them. They were working on a special Girl Scout badge that involved writing a history report about one of the presidents. Maryann's report was on Calvin Coolidge. She flipped through the C encyclopedia, but the only things she really bothered to look at were pictures of cats and the maps of California.

Charmaine, though she was glad to be in the company of a girl who was a year older, did not consider Maryann Hastings much of a historian. Though Charmaine hadn't done a lot of bragging about it, her report on Chester A. Arthur was a whole lot better than Maryann's. Maryann had barely even started hers, and furthermore, she didn't really seem all that interested in Calvin Coolidge.

Charmaine, who intended to get every single Girl Scout badge it was possible to get, decided to share some of her wisdom with Maryann. "My president, Chester A. Arthur, was sometimes called the gentleman boss. He was tall and handsome and traveled widely. As a lawyer in New York City, and later as president, he was a champion of civil rights."

Maryann was not even pretending to pay attention. All she was doing was looking out the window toward the back yard and fanning the pages of the encyclopedia.

She suddenly declared, "I'm so bored I could croak!" and slammed the book shut. "I don't care a diddly darn about Calvin Coolidge or Chester A. Arthur. All they are is a couple of dead guys!"

Charmaine was stupefied at this remark, although it did verify her suspicions. *Why had Maryann even bothered to come over to work on the report?* Before Charmaine could ask, Maryann added, "Let's talk about real, live people. For instance (she glanced back out the window, toward the Davy Crockett tent, and tried to make it sound as though his name had just occurred to her) tell me all about ... Bernie."

"Bernie!" said Charmaine. "Why do you want to know about Bernie?"

"Mmmm I don't know." Maryann picked at her fingernail. "I guess I just have a natural curiosity about people."

Charmaine shrugged her shoulders. "Well, he's my brother.

And I've always had to live with him. That's about it."

Maryann frowned at Charmaine and said, "What I mean is ... what kind of girls does he like?"

"Girls! You must be kidding! Bernie doesn't like girls. Bernie likes bugs and worms and snakes."

"Maybe he doesn't like girls now," said Maryann, "but when he does start to, what kind of girls do you think he'll like?"

"I don't know," said Charmaine. "Probably the creepy kind."

Maryann seemed offended.

Charmaine reconsidered. After all, she was his sister, so whatever Bernie did also reflected on her. "Actually," she confessed, "Bernie was in love once, and he still might be, with Miss Jamison. But you can't tell anyone, ever."

Maryann crinkled up her face. *Miss Jamison! She could never compete with Miss Jamison!* She sat up and folded her arms across her chest. "That's the dumbest thing I've ever heard," she said. "Boys can't be in love with their teachers."

An equally unpleasant look appeared on Charmaine's face. "I'm surprised you haven't figured it out by now, Maryann, but Bernie is not like other boys."

"I know," said Maryann, staring out the window, where he and Alex were having a contest to see who could spit further. Her voice got all soft. "I know."

✳✳✳✳✳✳✳✳✳✳

Maryann Hastings had never spent the night at Charmaine's house before, but that was the plan. Right now the two girls were on their way to the Hastings' house, because Maryann couldn't bear to spend the night away from Sweetie Pie, her big white poodle. As Maryann repeatedly pointed out, Sweetie Pie was a purebred, which made her smarter and better behaved than most dogs. When Sweetie Pie came prancing up the Jones's sidewalk, Weezer was immediately attracted to her.

He sprang from his doghouse, gave her a long serious sniff, then licked the side of her face. Sweetie Pie responded by growling ferociously and nipping the air just inches from his face. Charmaine took a step backward, as did Weezer. Maryann laughed and said, "Oh don't worry. She always does that."

While the boys roasted hotdogs in the backyard, the girls ate TV dinners in the living room, watching cartoons and the Mickey Mouse Club. Sweetie Pie obligingly sat at Maryann's feet, curled into a fluffy white ball, hoping for a handout. Weezer, who was outside with the boys, was definitely interested in the strange white dog, but he preferred the company of his beloved master and the campfire and the morsels of hotdog he occasionally received.

Thus, the evening progressed. When the TV dinners were eaten and the evening news began, Maryann suddenly said, "You know what I'd like? I'd like to have a marshmallow."

"I know where we can get some marshmallows," said Charmaine. "Bernie and Alex have a whole bag in the backyard."

Maryann's face lit up like a jack-o'-lantern. "Mmmm good idea."

Bernie and Alex had managed to get the temperature of their campfire right where they liked it, from the high heat of the hotdog roasting stage to red hot coals for dessert. They had just sharpened their sticks and were reaching into the bag of marshmallows when suddenly they spotted the girls sneaking around the corner of the house. Instinctively, the boys sprawled themselves flat on the ground and began throwing pine cones from the stacks they had gathered for just this purpose. Their number one rule when girls were lurking about: always be ready for warfare.

Charmaine was used to being bombarded with one thing or another by Bernie and Alex, so she showed Maryann how to run for cover, behind the apple tree. There, she started gathering up the softest, smooshiest apples she could find.

"What are we gonna do with these?" asked Maryann.

"Throw them at the boys, of course," said Charmaine.

Maryann looked down at the brown, rotting apples. "I don't want to throw these at Bernie."

"Why not?" asked Charmaine.

"Because ... because ... I love him."

Charmaine's mouth dropped wide open and all her apples fell to the ground. "I thought you hated him."

Maryann gave Charmaine a look that was intended to make her feel stupid. "That was yesterday."

Charmaine doubled over with laughter and said, "Boy oh boy oh boy! Bernie's gonna flip when he hears this!"

Maryann grabbed hold of Charmaine's sweater, glared into her eyes and said, "You have to promise me you won't tell him. Come on, promise! As a Girl Scout."

Charmaine refused to answer. She knew she had the upper hand and she wanted to play her cards just right.

"I know," said Maryann. "I'll give you something really good. Something you'll really really like."

"Oh all right," said Charmaine. After all, Maryann was a guest. She held up her hand and said, "Girl Scout's honor."

Maryann leaned in close and whispered in Charmaine's ear. "When Bernie and I get married, you can be the maid of honor and wear a beautiful frilly pink dress."

Charmaine did a double take. *Maryann wanted to marry Bernie!* Boy oh boy, that was definitely going into her notebook of interesting things. But all she said was, "What if I don't want to wear a frilly pink dress!"

"Well that's just too bad," snapped Maryann, who had spent many hours planning what the wedding party would wear. "It's my wedding and if I say you have to wear a frilly pink dress, then that's what you have to wear. Now let's go get some marshmallows."

Too stunned not to, Charmaine followed Maryann as she worked her way around the edge of the Jones's backyard, trying to dodge the flying pine cones. Just as the girls reached the campfire, the boys, with smirks on their faces, made a big show of officially dropping all their ammunition and giving each of the girls a marshmallow already on the stick and ready to roast.

"It's a peace offering," said Bernie.

"Thank you," Maryann told him. "I'll share it with you, if you like."

Alex laughed out loud, then quickly made his voice sound sincere. "Gee Maryann, that's nice of you."

"Uh, no thanks," said Bernie. "I've already had (he counted on his fingers) about twenty."

Charmaine knew her brother and Alex well enough; she should have been more suspicious, but her mind was occupied with what Maryann had just told her. Instead of inspecting the marshmallow the way she usually would have, she just stood there, roasting it to a golden brown, wondering if Maryann would let her wear a blue frilly dress to the wedding instead. She looked much better in blue.

Maryann, who had no brothers and who, everyone was astonished to discover, had never eaten a s'more before, was carefully roasting her marshmallow, rotating the stick just so, until the whole thing was a lovely shade of brown. Charmaine kept telling Maryann precisely how best to cook it while the boys stood by silently, smiling and shuffling their feet. At the same

43

moment, the girls popped their treats into their mouths and crunched down.

Bernie and Alex erupted with laughter and hoots and howls, as the girls were spitting out the remains of their marshmallows, gagging and coughing up brown goo.

"Mud!" yelled Charmaine. "You stuffed our marshmallows with mud!"

Bernie and Alex rolled around on the ground, laughing until tears streamed down their faces.

Maryann was furious. She was beyond furious. Just then Weezer and Sweetie Pie came bounding into the yard, covered from head to toe with (everybody smelled it at the same time) cow manure! Up the hill, the Johannsen family kept two milk cows on their property. On very special occasions, Weezer and some of the other dogs in the neighborhood liked to go up there and roll around in the cow droppings.

"I'm going home right this minute," Maryann said. "I can see this has all been a huge mistake."

Charmaine followed her to the edge of the yard.

"I'm sorry you didn't have a good time," Charmaine said. "I told you we should've attacked the boys with those rotten apples." She was starting to think Bernie had been right all along in his opinion of Maryann Hastings. How could a self-respecting Girl Scout pretend to be interested in Chester A. Arthur when she was really interested in Bernie Jones?

Maryann stomped her foot on the sidewalk. "Well, if Bernie thinks he can treat me like this and I'll still be in love with him, he's got another think coming. And if you ever breathe one single word about what I told you, to anyone, ever, even if you live to be a thousand years old, I'll … I'll … I don't know what I'll do, but it'll be the meanest, worst, most terrible thing you could ever imagine." She scrunched her face into a terrible frown.

Charmaine, who had never been outdone by a frown before, crisscrossed her heart and promised she would never, ever tell. Girl Scout's honor.

Maryann marched down the street, madder than she had ever been in her whole life, with Sweetie Pie, more brown than white, prancing happily alongside. Already Maryann was planning a series of mean things to do and say to Bernie. She paused for a moment to gaze up at the brightest star she could find, and made a wish that during the night a tornado would suck up the Davy Crockett tent, carry it all the way to the Sahara Desert and drop it into a big pit full of scorpions.

Bernie, meanwhile, was poking his roasting stick into the fire, stuffing a handful of marshmallows into his mouth and laughing at Alex's imitation of Chuckie Wadsworth. The muddied marshmallows were ancient history; the girls were far from their minds. It was Friday night, there was a sky full of stars and they were camping. Tomorrow they were going hiking in Peabody Gulch, and in the evening all their favorite programs were on TV. Bernie gave a quick thought to the years ahead. Life would have to improve a whole great big bunch to get any better than this.

The Field Trip

The instant Bernie awoke, he jumped out of bed. Oh boy ... this was a day he had been looking forward to for a long time. Today his class was going on a field trip to the museum. There would be a long bus ride to and from the city, the chance to look at all kinds of interesting stuff, and then the best part of the day: dinner at the all-you-can-eat Chuckwagon restaurant. Bernie put on his lucky shirt and ran downstairs.

Charmaine was sitting at the kitchen table with a big frown on her face. "Hmmph! I don't think it's the least bit fair that Bernie's class gets to go on a field trip and I have to have a regular old school day." She snarled up her face, stuck out her lower lip and stared at him until he finally returned her gaze, at which time she crossed her eyes. Then she reached across the table for some toast and accidentally on purpose spilled her orange juice on him.

Bernie ran to the sink and grabbed a dish towel. "My lucky shirt!" he shrieked. "You spilled juice on my lucky shirt!"

"I didn't mean to. And anyway, what's so lucky about your dumb old shirt? I wouldn't be caught dead in that ugly old brown thing!"

Bernie mopped himself off, debated whether or not to put on something else, and decided he'd better not. You never could tell what might happen; it was always best to have luck on your side.

"Now let me get this straight," said Mrs. Jones. "The bus leaves the school at 9:30 a.m., and we'll be back by 7:00 p.m. tonight?" She was going on the field trip, too, as a chaperone.

"Yep," said Bernie. "And Miss Jamison said we can sit with anyone on the bus. We don't have to sit with our buddy." At the start of the year Miss Jamison had informed the students that for all their field trips and excursions, they would use the buddy system. Bernie's buddy was Anne-Marie Williams, who sat beside him in class and had a habit of drumming her fingers on the side of her desk. Plus, she had the strange ability to make weird, squeaking noises in her throat, and often did. Plus, she was a girl.

Bernie didn't have to be concerned about that today because he'd be sitting with his real buddy, Alex. He gobbled down his breakfast, gathered up his books and ran out the door. His big day had officially begun.

Mrs. Jones rushed around getting ready for the field trip, when she was interrupted by a phone call. It was the hospital. There was an emergency, and all the blood donors of her type were being called in. She frowned, thought for a second, then picked up the phone and called the one person she knew would gladly take her place on the field trip, Grandpa Jones.

"Why sure," he told her from his room at the senior center. "I'll walk on up to the school and be there by 9:15 a.m."

✳✳✳✳✳✳✳✳✳✳

Bernie sat at his desk with a big smile on his face. Miss Jamison hadn't arrived yet, which was odd, because she was always the first one in the room. Just then the door opened, and in came the dreaded substitute teacher, Mrs. Broadbottom.

"Good morning!" she boomed in her loud voice. "Miss Jamison is ill today. But don't worry, you'll still have your tour through the museum." She glanced at the piece of paper in her hand. "Mrs. Jones and I will make sure that your day is both pleasurable and educational, although personally I believe your time would be much better spent in the classroom.

"By the way, there will be another change of plans. Today we will be using the buddy system. You will sit with your buddy. You will tour the museum with your buddy. At all times you will be close enough that when I say, 'Show me your buddy!' you will clasp your partner's hand and raise it high above your head. Am I making myself absolutely clear?"

Bernie's heart sank. Now he would have to sit with Anne-Marie Williams all the way to the city and walk with her through the museum and listen to her yacking and squeaking the whole time. Usually his lucky shirt prevented stuff like this from happening. *Oh well,* he told himself, *I'm not going to let her keep me from having a good time,* and when the big yellow bus pulled up in front of the school, the only thing he felt was excitement.

"I would like to know where Mrs. Jones is," Mrs. Broadbottom announced, in Bernie's direction. All he could do was shrug his shoulders as his face turned bright red. His mom wasn't usually late for stuff. Mrs. Broadbottom added, "I sincerely hope she's not lollygagging around, because if she is, she's going to make us late."

Just then a voice from the back of the room let out a long, loud chuckle. "Lollygagging. Now there's a word I haven't heard in a long time." Grandpa walked to the front of the class, smiling as he reached out to shake hands with the teacher.

"How do, Miss Jamison. My name's Augustus Jones, but you can call me Gus. I'm the granddad of that boy right there. His mother needs me to pinch hit for her today, and I'm rarin' to go."

Something about him, the twinkle in his eyes, his friendly smile, pleased Mrs. Broadbottom. "I'm very happy to meet you," she said. "However, I'm not Miss Jamison. I'm Beatrice Broadbottom, the substitute teacher."

"Well you and me are gonna have a good old time with this bunch today, I can tell you that," said Grandpa. "And if I'm not mistaken, that's our bus right there. Let's load 'em up and get this show on the road."

"Indeed," said Mrs. Broadbottom, smoothing back her hair. It had been many years since her dear husband passed away, and she missed the company of a gentleman. Perhaps the bus trip, which she had been dreading, wouldn't be so bad after all.

✳✳✳✳✳✳✳✳✳

Anne-Marie Williams talked nonstop for two solid hours. She told Bernie, in painful detail, every gift she got for Christmas, the names of all her dolls, her favorite TV shows and the many problems her mom and dad had with her big brother, Marvin. Since she was sitting by the window, Bernie mostly stared at the seat in front of them while his thoughts wandered far and wide.

Mrs. Broadbottom and Grandpa sat in one of the front seats and chatted quietly back and forth. About halfway to the city, without any warning, Mrs. Broadbottom suddenly turned around and shouted, "Show me your buddy!"

Panic overwhelmed the handful of students who had quietly switched seats. Instead of just holding up the hand of the person nearest them, they all tried to scramble back to their original seats, and for a moment there was complete chaos on the bus.

An enormous frown overtook Mrs. Broadbottom's face. She hoisted herself up from her seat and shouted, "I made it perfectly clear that I will not tolerate this kind of behavior. Next time, if you are not with your assigned partner, then (she paused for a moment, trying to decide which punishment would hurt the most) *you will not be allowed to eat at the Chuckwagon.* I am quite serious about this. Don't make me prove it." She squinted up her eyes and dropped to her seat in a graceless plunge, causing Grandpa to bounce partially out of his seat.

✳✳✳✳✳✳✳✳✳

After they had driven past corn fields and wheat fields and tiny little towns, the bus crossed a series of bridges, and the tall buildings of the city suddenly came into view. The disappointments of not having Miss Jamison on the trip and then having to sit with his buddy vanished, and once again Bernie was full of excitement.

I am on a bus, he said to himself. *I am traveling to the city, to see things I've never seen. Soon I'll be in a big museum and there'll be great stuff to look at all day.* It no longer mattered that he'd had to share his seat with Anne-Marie Williams. She wasn't really all that bad ... for a girl. He thought about Mrs. Broadbottom's stern warning, then out of the corner of his eye he looked at Anne-Marie and thought, *no matter what, I'm not letting you out of my sight.*

The bus pulled up to the front of the museum and all the kids lined up with their partners. "I expect you all to act like ladies and gentlemen," said Mrs. Broadbottom, firmly grasping Grandpa's arm.

Grandpa had decided that, once they were inside the museum, he would put some distance between himself and Mrs. Broadbottom. She was getting a little too friendly for him.

When Bernie stepped inside the huge building, it was so glorious, so grand, he could hardly believe it. He turned his head this way and that, to glimpse the long long hallway with its many rooms and all the balconies above.

Step step step step, the two lines lead by Mrs. Broadbottom and Grandpa made their way toward the visitor's desk. After they checked in, all the students would be given a chance to get a drink of water and visit the restroom before starting their tour.

Somehow that information escaped Anne-Marie Williams, who had only one thing on her mind: if she didn't get to the bathroom RIGHT NOW she was in big trouble. She saw a sign that said "Ladies," down one of the hallways they had just passed, so she did the only thing she could. She stepped out of line and, trying to make herself invisible, ran to the bathroom.

Oh no, thought Bernie, *what is she doing? Where is she going?* But he could only keep step step stepping along with everyone else and hope that she returned before Mrs. Broadbottom noticed.

A moment later, like a bad dream, Bernie heard the four little words that had the power to ruin his day. Mrs. Broadbottom halted the marchers, turned around and shouted, *"Show me your buddy!"*

As twelve pairs of hands shot into the air, Bernie instinctively hunkered down, shut his eyes and covered his head with his hands. *Where was Anne-Marie?*

Two thoughts ran through the head of Mrs. Broadbottom as she stood at the front of the line and scanned the hands that were held aloft. Something wasn't quite right back there, toward the end of the line. Perhaps she should go and see. Her other thought was for Grandpa, whom she was beginning to find more and more interesting as the minutes ticked away.

Presently Grandpa was gawking at a huge marble sculpture of a woman playing a violin. Who knows for what reason - maybe it was more comfortable - but she was not wearing a single stitch of clothing. Mrs. Broadbottom was of the opinion that everyone, at all times, should be fully clothed, even objects of art. Though she had begun to warm to Grandpa's oddball sense of humor, it perturbed her that anyone would openly stare at something so inappropriate, even in a museum. She crossed one hand over the other, held her head high and sniffed loud enough that Augustus could hear. With so much on her mind, she didn't notice the thin tiny sound: click click click click of Anne-Marie Williams, coming out of the ladies room, partially walking, partially running, desperate to rejoin her class.

Grandpa looked away from the violin-playing woman and saw Bernie hunkered into a ball, trying to hide himself. He

also saw Anne-Marie, sneaking down the hall. To distract Mrs. Broadbottom, Grandpa quickly pointed to the first thing he saw, a metal sculpture, and said, "Take a look at that, Beatrice!"

Mrs. Broadbottom was pleased that Grandpa had called her by her first name. She stared at the sculpture and thought, *what in the world is that thing?*

"What in the world *is* that thing?" Grandpa asked, scratching his jaw. "Whatever it is, it's a doozy."

Mrs. Broadbottom threw her head back and laughed, she felt so good, and in that instant, Anne-Marie slipped back into line and hooked hands with Bernie. His heart was pounding so hard, it felt like it was going to jump right out of his chest.

Mrs. Broadbottom turned, gave the class another scan and said, "All right, hands down." They all marched to the front desk, where they officially checked in.

A sophisticated gentleman named Pierre was their tour guide. Bernie could tell he was sophisticated because he wore a light blue suit with a matching tie, and he had managed to coax a pencil-thin mustache into place. He had also taken care to slick his few remaining strands of hair over to the side to cover the bald dome of his head.

Pierre knew exactly what interested fourth graders. He cracked a lot of jokes and told stories about the artists' lives, and now that Bernie wasn't scared out of his wits anymore, the museum tour was starting to be fun.

Around and around they strolled, past many wonderful paintings, photographs, sculptures; there were a jillion things to look at. Then, for Bernie, came the really good part: the history wing of the museum.

He loved all the displays, especially the ancient artifacts and the wax figures of people who had lived a long time ago. Pierre knew a whole lot about history, and he answered everyone's questions - even the really dumb ones - without ever making fun.

Bernie tried to keep an eye on Grandpa up there at the front of the line. It looked like he and Mrs. Broadbottom were getting along pretty well. She was laughing at whatever he was saying and smiling a lot. You'd almost think she was having a good time.

The truth was, Mrs. Broadbottom's feet were killing her. To sit down, far away from this tribe of noisy, curious children, was exactly what she wanted. She felt certain that even ten minutes would restore her. A nice cup of coffee would also help, and perhaps a doughnut or two. Touring a museum with twenty-six children was her least favorite way to spend a day, but her reputation as a substitute teacher was at stake, and she was determined to remain in a good humor. Plus she had few opportunities to meet men, especially ones as likeable as Augustus Jones. Certainly, he was not what you would call polished, but he was nevertheless extremely interesting.

Mrs. Broadbottom was certain that, buried beneath Grandpa's rough exterior, there was a gem, just waiting for some smart woman to come along and give a good polishing. The wheels of her mind clicked ahead full speed. *She would invite him to dinner. Their friendship would blossom. Who could tell what the future might hold?*

✳✳✳✳✳✳✳✳✳

Bernie loved the Wild West exhibit, with life-sized models of Buffalo Bill and Annie Oakley, with their shiny pistols and rifles, under a locked glass case near the cashier. There was also a sod house, just like the ones people lived in in olden times. With no difficulty, Bernie could imagine what it was like, living in the sod house, shooting one of the shiny pistols. Miss Jamison had been right ... touring the museum *did* make history come alive, and Bernie loved it. If it wasn't for the fact that their next stop was the all-you-can-eat Chuckwagon buffet, he would have wanted to spend the whole rest of his life in the museum.

From out of nowhere, while Pierre was explaining the many hardships of the pioneers' long journey westward, Chuckie Wadsworth suddenly whispered, "Hey Bern, how about lettin' me see your ring."

Bernie instinctively covered his left hand with his right. His Captain Marvel whistling ring was his favorite possession and the object of envy for all the kids. He had spent three whole dollars on it and had waited six long weeks for it to arrive in the mail from the cereal company. No way did he want to take it off his finger and let anyone handle it, especially Chuckie Wadsworth. He pretended he hadn't heard.

"Hey Bernie! Are you deaf? Let me see your ring!" Chuckie whispered so loud that half the class heard him.

Pierre was trying to explain how well-constructed the Conestoga wagons were, and how the settlers could only pack their most prized belongings.

Mrs. Broadbottom began to fidget; she could hear whispers from the back of the line. Bernie's eyes were trained on her and, in order to keep her from turning around, he reluctantly took off his ring and handed it to Chuckie.

Bernie had known Chuckie Wadsworth all his life. Chuckie seemed to live in a world of his own, and was forever being sent to the principal's office. He now put the Captain Marvel whistling ring on his finger, took it off, put it back on, took it off, put it back on, pretended he was going to blow it, then got an evil smile on his face and casually tossed it into the back of the Conestoga wagon, where it rolled in amongst the many household possessions of some long ago pioneer family.

Uhhh! Bernie sucked in a whole chest full of air. His ring! It was gone! What could he do? He turned to face Chuckie with rage in his eyes, but Chuckie, along with the rest of the class, was marching on to view the next display.

Bernie was in shock. *What should he do?* There was no time to decide; he could only act. Carefully, quietly, he slipped out of line and around to the back of the wagon. Before he could decide not to, he climbed inside.

Wow! It was really cool in there, all that really old stuff: a butter churn, a pump organ and a doll that must have been a hundred years old. It was so neat, it was almost worth the risk he was taking. Bernie wanted to stay and admire all the rest of the old stuff, but he had to get his ring and get out of there

fast. He dropped to his knees and frantically began searching through the many layers of straw on the wagon floor. Trying not to panic, his fingers frantically searching through the layers of straw, Bernie realized a terrible truth: *he would never be able to find his ring.*

As luck would have it, Mrs. Broadbottom, in her extra-loud voice, shouted, "Show me your buddy!" Bernie scrambled to get out of the covered wagon, but his shoelace became hooked on a pitchfork, and when he tried to get it out, the pitchfork fell on his head. It was heavy, and it hurt so bad, Bernie couldn't stop himself from hollering, "Ouch!"

Pierre came running. Mrs. Broadbottom and Grandpa came running. The whole class gathered around the Conestoga wagon and stared in disbelief. Half the students wondered the very same thing: *why in the world would Bernie Jones do something that would so obviously get him into trouble?*

By then Bernie had managed to get his foot free and climb back out of the wagon. There was a big red welt on the side of his head. Grandpa hurried to put his arms around his grandson, and it was all Bernie could do to keep from bursting into tears. "My ring," he blubbered into Grandpa's ear, "I was looking for my ring."

"Please take these children on to the next display," Mrs. Broadbottom said to Pierre. "I will deal with this boy." Grandpa held Bernie at arm's length and gave him a long, serious look that ended in a smile, which made Bernie feel that maybe, just maybe, everything would be okay. Then he released Bernie to Mrs. Broadbottom, who lead him to the back of the room.

There was a bench there, and they both sat down. At first, Mrs. Broadbottom wanted to shake the living daylights out of Bernie, or at least box his ears, but she knew that Grandpa was watching. She closed her eyes and told herself, *just calm down, Beatrice. This too shall pass.*

"All right, young man, I would like an explanation." Then she leaned in closer and added, "and it better be a good one. I made it perfectly clear before we left the school that if anyone caused any trouble, that person would not be allowed to join the rest of us at the Chuckwagon for dinner. Is that what you would like, to remain on the bus while the rest of us dine?'"

Stay on the bus! Not go to the Chuckwagon! The thought of missing out on all that fried chicken and pizza and spaghetti and ice cream hurt Bernie a lot worse than the bump on his head or even the loss of his whistling ring. He shook his head no and sniffed back a tear.

Under normal circumstances, Bernie would never tell on another kid. Anyone else in his class, if they had done the thing Chuckie Wadsworth had done, would be severely punished. But there was a special set of rules that seemed to apply only to Chuckie, everyone knew that. Though he wasn't exactly sure what or how much he should say, Bernie took a deep breath, and told the story exactly as it had happened.

Mrs. Broadbottom, who was starving, and oh so glad to be off her feet, listened to every word Bernie said. *It was so nice to be away from those noisy children and all their endless questions.* To buy herself a few more minutes of peace, when Bernie was done she asked him to repeat the entire story.

She took it all in, in a most interested way. As a substitute teacher, over the years Mrs. Broadbottom had seen so many things, so very many things. She had no trouble imagining the young hooligan, Chuckie Wadsworth, demanding the ring of a nice boy like Bernie, then tossing it into a Conestoga wagon. She smiled at Bernie and patted the bruise on the side of his head.

It hurt a little when she did that, but Bernie was so relieved she wasn't mad at him, he didn't mind.

By the time Bernie and Mrs. Broadbottom caught up with the rest of the class, they were at the futuristic display, which included a real space capsule. It was rumored that every now and then the museum people allowed a kid to sit in it, if they were especially good.

"How about it, Mrs. Broadbottom?" asked Pierre. "Is there a special child you would like to honor today?"

The other kids were shocked when Mrs. Broadbottom said, "As a matter of fact, there is," and pointed to Bernie Jones.

Word had gotten around about what Chuckie had done, and when the announcement was made, all the other kids burst into applause. Bernie's face flushed with pride. *A real space capsule!* Mrs. Broadbottom beamed at Grandpa, who for the first time all day thought, *she's a handful but maybe she's not so bad after all.*

Bernie got to put on the astronaut's helmet and sit in the astronaut's chair and adjust all the knobs and dials in the space capsule. Pierre took his picture and everyone treated him like he was a hero.

The whole class got back on the bus and drove to the Chuckwagon. There they stuffed themselves with fried chicken and pizza and spaghetti and macaroni and cheese and jello salad with marshmallows and dozens of other things. When everyone was so full they could hardly move, they all made huge ice cream sundaes, with chocolate and cherries and walnuts and whipped cream piled six inches high.

Instead of stuffing herself the way she had planned, Mrs. Broadbottom attempted to impress Grandpa by nibbling strictly on salad and yogurt. Afterward, she was so pleased with herself, she announced that the students could sit anywhere they wanted on the bus; no more buddy system today.

With his best friend by his side, and the memory of being in the space capsule forever burned into his brain, Bernie said a thing he would never say to anyone else in the whole world except Alex, "Know what? I feel just like a king! And I owe it all to my lucky shirt."

Alex glanced at Bernie's juice-stained shirt and silently nodded in agreement.

Mrs. Broadbottom was feeling pretty special herself. She secretly hoped the bus would break down or have a flat tire so she could have a little more time with Augustus Jones.

Grandpa, who was stuffed to the gills, and whose feet also hurt, could see there was trouble on the horizon. He was no stranger to romance. He could tell when a woman was starting to take a shine to him, and this one definitely was. He didn't like to hurt anyone's feelings, but he'd have to let her know pretty quickly that he wasn't interested. He stared out the window and wondered what to do.

Mrs. Broadbottom launched into a long story about her childhood, which worked its way around to the many difficulties of her job. "I'm just thankful this day went as well as it did. And thank goodness the children aren't singing. In my many years of teaching I have learned it is the one thing that, once it gets started, is impossible to control on a bus."

Grandpa instantly saw a way out of his problem. He whispered to his seat mate, "I'm sorry Beatrice. I guess I'll always be a kid at heart, but it's been so long since I've heard this song, I just can't help myself." He then stood up, took a deep breath, turned to face the rear of the bus, and belted out in a voice that was immediately joined by twenty-six others: "99 bottles of beer on the wall, 99 bottles of beer, take one down, pass it around, 98 bottles of beer on the wall!"

The Disappearance of King George

Weezer, curled up on Bernie's bed, was having a miserable time trying to sleep. He rolled to the right, closed his eyes and waited for sleep to overtake him. When it did not, he rolled to the left and waited again. Back and forth, back and forth. Usually all he had to do in order to fall asleep was to close his eyes. Tonight was different though. After what seemed like hours, he heard the sound of raindrops blasting the side of the house and the maple trees in the back yard swaying in the wind.

As Bernie continued to sleep, Weezer eased himself down from the bed and went to stand at the window. Normally, in and of itself, a storm would not cause him any distress. But this particular morning, Weezer had a strong feeling that something was wrong. He had no idea what it was, but he was certain that something, somehow, somewhere was wrong.

He gazed out the window for a while, then returned to the bed, where he stared mournfully at his master. Soon he began making the tiniest squeak, way down deep in his throat, a sound which he had not planned to make, but which came out naturally, as a result of whatever bad thing was happening.

When Bernie awakened, Weezer's face was six inches from his, and the squeaking had become much louder, so that right away Bernie knew something was wrong.

"What is it, boy?" he asked, rubbing his eyes with his fists.

When Weezer's squeaking got even louder, Bernie tromped down the stairs and opened the front door. Like a cannon, Weezer shot out of it and disappeared down the street. Exhaling a yawn so wide it almost dislocated his jaw, Bernie returned to bed and was asleep within moments.

Two blocks away, desperately longing for sleep, Mr. Cunningham, who worked from 3:00 p.m. until 11:00 p.m. at the paper mill, stood in his kitchen staring into his back yard, watching for his little chihuahua, King George. When he had come home from work, Georgie was not in his usual place on the porch. Because this had happened once or twice before, Mr. Cunningham decided he'd have a midnight snack, get ready for bed and surely by then the king would be home.

He fixed himself a ham sandwich and watched the late news on TV. He waited for Georgie for about half an hour, read a chapter from his book, waited another half hour or so, but still King George did not return. Finally, Mr. Cunningham went to bed.

What no one knew - because no one had seen it happen - was that earlier that evening, King George had more or less been kidnapped.

It had begun like any other evening. Georgie was lazing on the

front porch, bored, wishing he had something to do. Suddenly he heard a sound in the distance, which he knew for certain was the chattering of a squirrel. He listened more closely and was able to identify its precise location: the Morton's oak tree, a block and a half away. Excited and pleased to have a mission, Georgie scampered down the steps and hurried toward the sound.

Along with most of the pets in the neighborhood, all his life King George had wanted to catch a squirrel. He had been told the taste of squirrel was similar to the taste of chicken, which he knew was tasty indeed.

Like his best friend, Weezer, King George was not the smartest dog in the world, and he had no idea what he would do with a squirrel, a creature almost half his size. He had a vague plan, once the killing was over, to have a small meal, then drag the rest of the carcass home, where he could show it off to the other neighborhood dogs and treat them all to a bite. As he hurried down the street, Georgie's happiness grew and grew. He would take the squirrel by surprise. He would wrestle it to a position where it could not fight back. After enjoying a few bites, he would bark triumphantly for an hour or so, then return home and curl up on his rug to await his master.

What King George did not count on was the new tenant in the Vine Street apartments, Mrs. O'Callaghan. Lately, she had been increasingly more confused about things. Frequently, when she paced around her new apartment, it didn't seem at all familiar. Was this really her house, Charles' and her house? When had they moved here? She would like to have asked Charles, but he was off on a business trip and she couldn't recall when he was supposed to be home.

As Mrs. O'Callaghan puzzled over all the changes that had recently taken place, a sudden movement outside the window caught her eye. A dog. A chihuahua. *It was Wally! Dear little Wally!* It had been such a long time since she had seen him! She might be uncertain about lots of things lately, but she would never be uncertain about Wally.

She grabbed her jacket, hurried to the door and took off down the street.

"Wally!" she shouted. "Come back, Wally!"

King George kept pitter-pattering down the street, his toenails clicking on the sidewalk, pleased that he was on such an important mission. When he heard Mrs. O'Callaghan shout, he glanced over his shoulder and, overcome with curiosity, decided to see what she was doing.

To his surprise, she headed straight toward him. He politely cocked his head to the side, to let her know that even though he was a danger to squirrels, he would never be so rude as to harm a hu-man.

"Oh my dear sweet little Wally!" Mrs. O'Callaghan said, scooping him up in her arms and heading back to her apartment, forgetting that Wally had been dead for more than ten years.

King George was astonished by her action, but she seemed so nice, he decided this was part of the evening's adventure. There was still plenty of time for catching squirrels.

"I've been so worried about you, Wally!" said Mrs. O'Callaghan. "I thought you were never coming back! It seems like it's been years since I've seen you. But never mind about that. How about I cook you your favorite - a nice juicy steak - when we get home?"

King George did not understand the word 'steak,' but when it was placed in front of him, he got the message. It was delicious! He had no idea that such things even existed. His human always fed him dry dog food. Because he hadn't known there *was* anything else, he had always been happy with what he had been served.

After the meal, when he was so stuffed he could barely walk, Mrs. O'Callaghan picked him up and carried him to the couch, where she held him on her lap and gave him a thorough scratching behind his ears.

"Just wait until your father comes home, Wally!" she said. "He'll be so happy to see that his little dog has returned. I hate to tell you this, but he gave you up for lost a long time ago. In fact, he tried to talk me into getting another dog, but I wouldn't even consider it. For me there is only one dog, and that is my dear sweet little Wally." She nuzzled her nose into the fur on King George's head. "I knew some day you'd find your way home." She began to softly hum all the lullabies she knew, cradling the dog until he happily fell asleep.

He slept a long time. It was well after midnight when King George awoke and discovered that a bed had been made for him: a green satin pillow on the floor. Next to it was a water bowl, and next to that was a dish of something else he had never eaten before ... canned dog food. He sniffed at it suspiciously. It wasn't quite as good as the steak, but it was good enough. He gobbled it all down, lapped up a little of the water, curled up on the green satin pillow and immediately fell back asleep.

That was right about the time that Mr. Cunningham decided to stop waiting for King George and to try to get some sleep. With a heavy heart, he climbed into bed, said a prayer for Georgie's safe return and stared at the ceiling for a long time, hoping for the relief that sleep would bring.

Now, since dawn, Mr. Cunningham had been out on the porch, pacing back and forth, whistling and calling, trying not to think about all the bad things that can happen to pets who all their lives have only been treated with love and kindness. A trusting dog like Georgie could get into a lot of trouble if he ended up trusting the wrong sort of person.

Starved of sleep and on the verge of tears, Mr. Cunningham pulled out his handkerchief and blew into it loudly. Just then Weezer appeared, making the first of his daily rounds of the neighborhood. He was still burdened by his feeling of worry, which, as he came closer to the Cunningham's house, grew into a huge ball of worry. When he heard fear in the voice of King George's human, Weezer knew he was getting close to the source of the problem. Scampering into the Cunningham's yard, he knew instantly that his little friend was not there.

"Weezer!" said Mr. Cunningham. "You haven't seen Georgie, have you? He wasn't here when I came home from work! I was sure he'd show up this morning, but he's still gone. I'm sick with worry!"

Weezer, who only knew a few human words, did not understand Georgie's master, who spoke quickly and waved his arms

70

frantically. Weezer did, however, understand the look on the human's face and what it meant in regard to Georgie's absence.

Sitting quite still, trying to look intelligent, Weezer woofed one small bark.

Despite the huge lump in his throat, Mr. Cunningham managed to say the thing that worried him the most, "What if he was hit by a car!"

Weezer barked another single bark, which was both loud and sad. *Car* was a word he understood.

Over the years, Mr. Cunningham and Weezer had a long, complicated relationship. Many times, Mr. Cunningham had considered putting up a fence to keep the dog once and forever out of his yard, but the frisky, friendly mutt brought so much joy to Georgie's life, the soft-hearted human could not bring himself to do it. Having Weezer in his yard at this, his hour of need, brought Mr. Cunningham a good deal of comfort, and he reached down to pet the dog's head, a head which many times he had claimed did not contain a brain. He reminded himself that earlier that morning, he made a promise that if and when his beloved Georgie returned, he would never scold either dog again.

Weezer gave out one more woof, then ran out of the yard. Mr. Cunningham, barely able to speak, said, "Find him for me, will you, Weezer? I promise, I'll never yell or throw apple cores at you again." At his wits end, with no one on the street to see, he dropped his head and let his tears flow.

Without knowing where to search, Weezer's instincts lead him to Pine Street. As luck would have it, right outside the tallest building on the block, there was King George, on the leash of a gray-haired woman whom Weezer had never seen before.

He barked with relief to see Georgie and ran straight toward him. The small brown dog, who by now was almost as confused as Mrs. O'Callaghan, returned Weezer's greeting and strained against the leash to get away.

"No, no Wally!" scolded Mrs. O'Callaghan from underneath her umbrella. "Now that you're back home, we don't want you wandering away again!" Then she promptly lead him back to her apartment and herded him inside. He barely managed to get a string of yips out to Weezer before she closed the door, but his message had been clear: "Get Bernie! Get Bernie! Get Bernie!"

Of course! Bernie would know what to do! As fast as his legs could carry him, Weezer ran toward Park Street, then up two blocks and down the alley to his home.

Bernie was sitting at the kitchen table, eating a bowl of Rice Krispies and studying the back of the cereal box. Weezer ran to the window, threw his head back and barked out the story of King George's kidnapping by a gray-haired lady on Pine Street.

Bernie did not understand what all the barking meant, but he knew that Weezer was desperate to communicate with him. He set down his spoon, grabbed his rain jacket and headed out the door.

As soon as he got outside, a gust of wind nearly blew him off his feet, plus it was raining much harder than it had appeared from the warm and cozy kitchen. "It's really stormy out here, Weezer!" Bernie shouted. "Are you sure this can't wait?" But Weezer was already halfway down the street, barking over his shoulder for Bernie to hurry up.

On and on they ran. In a few minutes Weezer lead his master directly to an apartment house on Vine Street, where he stood on the sidewalk and barked louder than he had ever barked before.

Every so often, in between Weezer's barks, Bernie could hear another dog inside the building; it was really more of a yip than a bark. Then the door opened and out ran King George, followed by someone he had seen before ... someone Bernie knew, but also didn't know.

King George ran straight for Weezer and began romping with his old pal. All the while the gray-haired lady scolded, "Wally! Come back here! Wally, come back!"

"Excuse me, Ma'am," said Bernie, "but that dog's name is King George. He lives in a white house right over there, with Mr. Cunningham."

The gray-haired lady smiled and said, "I'm afraid you're mistaken. Wally is my dog. I've had him for fifteen years. Charles and I got him when he was a puppy. We were living in Vermont at the time."

Then a shadow passed over her face, followed by a frown, and Bernie remembered who she was. A long time ago he and Alex had been on a penny hike downtown, and they had seen a lady come out of one of the shops with a confused look on her face. She had sat down on a bench and, for no apparent reason, began to cry. Bernie, because he couldn't bear to see someone suffer and do nothing, had gone to see if she needed some help. It turned out that she couldn't remember where she had parked her car. So Bernie and Alex treated her to an ice cream cone and included her in their penny hike. The three of them had walked around town until finally they found her car.

"I know you," the lady said, with a big smile. "You're the boy who helped me downtown, when I couldn't find my car."

"Yip," he said, offering out his hand. "My name's Bernie Jones and this is my dog Weezer. He came home just now, all worried about something. He wanted me to follow him, and that's why we're here." He added, "I hate to tell you this, but this isn't your dog." He gave her an apologetic smile. "I wish he were ... but he's not."

Mrs. O'Callaghan took several steps backward and studied the dog with every bit of her concentration. "Well goodness me, of course he's not Wally. I don't know what I was thinking. If he were Wally, he'd have to be, let's see (she started counting on her fingers) ... more than twenty-five years old. Everyone knows dogs don't live that long.

"Did I ever tell you about Wally?" she went on to say. "He was the sweetest, smartest little dog. When Charles brought him home to me, he could fit in the palm of my hand. We took that dog everywhere we went. He was like a child to us."

"Well," said Bernie, "I'd like to hear more about Wally, but I think I'd better get Georgie back to Mr. Cunningham. He's really worried about him."

"I can't tell you how pleased I am that you stopped by," said Mrs. O'Callaghan. "Now that you know where I live, some-day you and your friend Alex must pay me a visit. We'll have a nice cup of tea. And cookies, of course."

"That'd be great," said Bernie, who was surprised she had re-called Alex's name. Apparently she remembered some things pretty well and other things not at all. He picked up King George and started down the street.

"Be sure to come back and visit me!" she shouted.

"Don't worry," Bernie hollered. "I will. I'll bring Alex with me, and I'll bet Mr. Cunningham will let us borrow King George, so it'll be like seeing Wally again."

"Oh that would be so splendid," she said, her eyes sparkling. "I can't think of anything I would enjoy more."

Five minutes later Bernie was walking into Mr. Cunningham's yard, and Georgie was jumping out of his arms, running up the porch steps to see his master.

"Georgie! You little dickens! I was worried sick about you!" said Mr. Cunningham, as he bent to pick up his dog. "Where in the world were you?" Two fat tears rolled down his cheeks.

Pleased to be the center of so much attention, King George yipped out his story, though Weezer was the only one who un-derstood. Luckily, Bernie was there to tell it in human words.

"Mrs. O'Callaghan is a really nice lady," Bernie said, when Georgie finished his story. "But I think sometimes she gets a little confused."

"Well, he's home and safe, that's all that matters," said Mr. Cunningham, and with that he set King George on the lawn.

"I'll never be able to thank you enough, Bernie" said Mr. Cunningham. "And from now on, Weezer is welcome to come over and chase my squirrels and bark his head off, anytime day or night. That was the deal I made last night, when I was praying for Georgie's safe return, and I intend to keep my end of the bargain."

As Bernie headed down the street, another storm cloud broke, and a big gust of wind nearly knocked him off his feet again. The weather, however, was of no consequence to him. He felt so good, he laughed out loud. Having King George home safely and the second chance encounter with Mrs. O'Callaghan filled him with a feeling that life was good, and that this was the start of a perfectly perfect day.

Dreamer's Gift

Crouched in the upper branches of the Jones's apple tree, Dreamer the cat surveyed the world below. The tree was full of bright red apples and beneath it, the lawn stretched out like a thick green carpet, large and lovely, perfect for a cat to slink and slither through on her prowls around the yard.

Distracted by the thought of how grand her kingdom was, Dreamer was caught off guard by a sparrow, who flitted down from a branch above her. By the time she pounced for it, it hopped back into the sky and flew away.

To reassure herself that she hadn't really wanted that particular bird in the first place, she gave a quick toss of her head and squinted her eyes defiantly against the sun.

Dreamer had never caught a squirrel, but lately the idea of it was more and more on her mind. It was rumored that the Mc-

Quire's tomcat, Henry, who was among the best hunters in the neighborhood, no longer ate mice; he dined only on squirrels. It made Dreamer furious to think of the big orange tabby cat turning his nose up at the fat and furry mice she and all the other cats loved to eat. *He certainly is a conceited, egotistical beast,* she decided. *He probably considers himself better than all the other cats. In which case he is also a fool, because everyone knows that I am far superior when it comes to brains, beauty and speed.*

She extended her claws, dug them deeply into the apple tree, and quickly gave herself a manicure. If - as she hoped - any other cat were to glance into the tree, they would have to admit, she was not just an ordinary cat sitting in a tree, watching the world go by. She was special. She was outstanding. She was the Queen. Not that she cared for the opinions of other cats.

Another sparrow flitted by. This one hovered just out of reach, trying to make up its mind whether or not to land. Dreamer drew herself into a compact unit of speed and cunning, leaped forward, missed the bird, missed the branch and landed on a lower limb in a graceless position. *Well,* she said to herself, *imagine that. Now I am here, whereas I used to be there, but since I never make mistakes, this surely must be where I intended to be.* She nibbled at the tips of her paws, and told herself, *yes, this is much better, and surely I will catch the next bird that flies by.*

On the opposite side of the yard, attached by his leash to a long line and feeling miserable, was the Jones's dog, Weezer. True, he had plenty of room to run, and a wooded area in which to do his private business, and a spacious doghouse in which to sleep, but right now he lacked the one thing that made life worth living ... the family.

The family was in Fairfield for the weekend. They'd packed up their old Ford station wagon and left on Friday morning. Unlike most of the trips they took, though, this time Weezer had to stay behind.

The last thing Bernie had done before he jumped in the car was attach Weezer's leash to the line, pour him more food than any dog could possibly eat in two days, fill an enormous bowl with water, hug him an extra long time and promise to bring him back something extra special. When Mr. Jones beeped the horn, Bernie hurried to the car, rolled down the window and waved and shouted until the house was out of sight, "See ya Weezer! See ya! We won't be gone long! I'll miss you! Be a good dog! "

At first Weezer's tail had thumped at the sound of his two favorite words: good and dog. But when he saw the car backing out of the driveway and realized he was not in it, his tail began to sag. He soon sank to his belly and moped for the rest of the day.

From the apple tree, Dreamer observed Weezer's unhappiness, which cheered her enormously. She understood exactly what was happening. Earlier that morning, when the family began packing and shuttling suitcases out to the car, she had sat on the walkway, pretending to observe a trickle of ants as they made their way from one concrete square to another. In fact, she was observing the family: the legs as they hurried past, the hands clutching backpacks, boxes of animal crackers and books. She knew what they were up to, and to show them she didn't care, she flopped onto the walkway on her back and moved back and forth a bit, allowing the rough concrete to give her a thorough scratching.

"Dreamer! Go someplace else and roll around!" Mrs. Jones had warned her, after nearly tripping over the huge calico cat. *How very rude!* Dreamer remarked to herself, hunkering on the walkway, making herself smaller but still refusing to budge. *These humans, with their constant need to get in their big*

machine and go away! They ought to spend more time at home, so they can appreciate the finer things of life, such as their beautiful black, orange and white cat.

She hated that once again, for a day or two or three, there would be no one to brush her or pet her, no laps to sit in, no handouts from the dinner table. *Fine*, she told herself, *they don't need me and I don't need them.* While they finished packing the car, she strutted across the alley to the Baxter's house, curled up in a sunny spot on their porch and refused to even glance in the family's direction.

When Weezer saw all the action, he assumed he would be part of it. He wagged his tail in joyful anticipation of jumping in the car, settling himself in back with the children and watching the sights go by. That's why it was such a disappointment, being left behind.

Dreamer jumped down from the apple tree, strolled across the lawn and made her way toward the doghouse. Weezer was grateful for some company, even if it was his old enemy, the cat. He watched her approach and hoped she would be nice, instead of the way she usually was.

Everyone knows that dogs and cats do not speak the same language. They do, however, communicate quite well with an complicated system of looks and gestures. In order to taunt him to the fullest extent, Dreamer had to descend the tree, run across the yard, and stare deeply into his eyes until he finally gave up and looked at her. She could now express more complicated thoughts. A thousand times - at least - Weezer had told himself he would no longer be tricked into looking at the cat, who never had anything nice to say and had made his life miserable since the days of his puppyhood.

"Too bad you have to be tied up like this," she told him with her bright green eyes. "If the people really loved you, the way they love me, they would turn you loose."

Weezer exhaled a sigh and pretended not to hear her.

"Have you ever considered what might happen if the house catches on fire?" she asked, with a flick of her whiskers. "Or if the trees catch fire? You, I'm afraid, would be trapped. As for me, I will scamper up another tree and watch the whole glorious thing."

With that, she ran away, streaking across the lawn, twitching her tail back and forth to remind him that she was superior to him in every way.

She noticed a squirrel halfway up the Patterson's big spruce tree, staring off into space, contentedly munching on a cone. *Aha*, Dreamer thought, *here is my opportunity*. She crept silently to the base of the tree and began her ascent, slowly, soundlessly, never once taking her eyes off the distracted squirrel. When she reached the branch on which it stood, Dreamer involuntarily began to chatter aloud, the way she always did when she hunted birds (which is why she rarely caught one). For reasons she did not understand, mice did not inspire this same urge; she just pounced on them. The sound of her voice surprised not only her, but the squirrel as well, so he had plenty of time to get away. He easily scurried to a much higher branch, where he scolded her furiously and called her nasty names.

Discouraged and depressed, Dreamer clawed her way down the tree, hurried down the hill toward Peabody Gulch and savagely attacked the first fat, brown mouse she could find.

Weezer, meanwhile, was stretched out on his side, trying to think of what he should do. The family had been away for a full day, and all he had done was mope and fret and feel sorry for himself. Now it was evening. With the long night ahead of him, he decided that, to take his mind off his troubles, he should begin a project.

One of the things Weezer loved to do most was dig holes. Generally he avoided digging, though, because experience had taught him that humans do not like it when dogs dig holes in their yard. In order to be a good dog and avoid the scorn of the people, Weezer tried to resist the temptation to dig. But now that the thought was so solidly in his mind, and since the people were gone and couldn't possibly observe him, it didn't seem like it would be so bad if he dug one or two teeny tiny holes.

The thought of it instantly cheered him up. Now he had a purpose. In preparation, he wolfed down a king-sized portion of his food, lapped up a quart or so of water, selected a patch of lawn and started in.

Ah, to feel the earth give way beneath his paws! To place his nose in the freshly churned dirt and take a long, deep whiff. These were sensations so strong; even though the family was gone, life could still be good.

Down in Peabody Gulch, Dreamer was enjoying a two-course dinner: a fat, brown vole, topped off by a pointy-nosed shrew.

Stuffed to overflowing, flopped out on the grass, an idea occurred to her: *Whenever the people came home from a journey, they were always hungry and rushed to stare at the contents of the big cold box in the kitchen. Perhaps the family would appreciate a delicious mousey snack of their own.* The more she thought about it, the more certain she was that the family would love a little tidbit when they arrived home.

Dreamer was a little slow, on account of having overeaten, but soon enough another chubby mouse crept from his hiding place in search of food, and in the next instant Dreamer had him between her paws. She then made another spur of the moment decision ... that a live mouse would be ever so much more appealing than a dead mouse. Served live, the family could also have the pleasure of the kill.

She ran back up the hill toward home. When she reached the house, she scampered through her cat door to the basement, up the stairs, and into the kitchen. There she was confronted with a dilemma. If she let the mouse go, it would run and hide, and the humans would be deprived of their treat. Hmmm, she thought, looking around to consider her options.

She then did a thing she never did ... unless it was late at night and the people were in bed: she jumped onto the kitchen counter, where she immediately saw the solution she was seeking. *The sink! The sink was much too deep for a mouse to climb out of. Even this fat fellow cradled in her jaws couldn't leap out of this sink.* Dreamer spat the worried mouse into the basin, crept back along the counter, paused to nibble on a chunk of butter, then jumped down and went back outside.

In the yard, a mysterious sound caught Dreamer's attention.

She glanced over her shoulder. What she saw made her smile her smuggest smile. There was Weezer, in the far corner of the lawn, contentedly digging one hole after another.

Ha! thought Dreamer, *wait until the humans see this! He'll be banished to the doghouse forever. They might even give him away!*

All the way down to the gulch she savored the thought of how the people would react when they saw the holes in the yard. She thought, also, of how they would rejoice when they saw the delicious snack she had brought them. All evening she sat in the tall grass of Peabody Gulch, not willing to capture just any old mouse, but awaiting the fattest, juiciest ones.

Before long she had managed to catch two more. Each time she brought one into the house and dropped it in the sink, she experienced a marvelous feeling of satisfaction. It was like gazing at a Thanksgiving feast. She was so pleased with the results of her hard work, she curled up on the kitchen counter and fell sound asleep.

As Weezer settled into his doghouse for the evening, he felt a similar feeling of satisfaction, looking out at what he had accomplished: an even dozen holes, scattered randomly along the edge of the yard, each one at least a foot deep. He'd had so much fun, he'd lost track of time, and now he felt over-whelmingly tired. With his last bit of energy, he scratched his ear with his hind foot and tried to remember, *did I plan to dig so many holes?* Oh well, they looked good, with a cone-shaped pile of dirt alongside each one. It didn't occur to him to wonder how the family would react to his project. It was all he could do now to perform his nightly ritual: circle three times on his blanket, exhale a huge yawn, drop into a heap and await the magic of sleep to overtake him.

✳✳✳✳✳✳✳✳✳✳

The Jones family left Fairfield early the next morning and pulled into their driveway an hour after sunrise. Weezer, who would liked to have had a couple more hours of sleep, nonetheless sprang from his doghouse, ran across the yard and waited on the walkway for the family to emerge from the car. All four doors opened at the same time, with children and suitcases and pillows spilling everywhere, everyone talking at once and the general commotion that always accompanied the Jones family.

Mr. Jones stayed outside, unpacking the rest of the luggage. Bernie gave Weezer a new red rubber ball and rolled around on the grass with him. Thirsty for a drink of cold water, Mrs. Jones and Charmaine rushed straight to the kitchen.

The first shout that could be heard outside was from Mrs. Jones. "Dreamer!" she yelled. "Bad cat! Off the counter!" She clapped her hands in Dreamer's face, a rude gesture which made the cat want to scratch her. A few seconds later, Mrs. Jones and Charmaine were close enough to see what awaited them in the sink: three fat and furry mice, jumping and scrambling over each other, trying desperately to get away from whatever horror awaited them.

It seemed impossible that the nonstop screams and shrieks, which were so loud they woke all the neighbors, could have been made by only two people.

To prove she had committed no crimes, Dreamer took far more space than she needed on the walkway and groomed her coat, ignoring the humans as they walked back and forth with their possessions. She consoled herself with the thought that, when they discovered all the holes the dog had dug, it would more than even the score.

After a while Dreamer noticed, from the top of the car, the big human had unloaded ... what was it ... trees? Very small trees? Each one came up to the big human's middle and was wrapped in a bag full of dirt.

"Take a look at these, boy!" Bernie said to Weezer. "Our very own Christmas trees! We're going to plant them all along the edge of our yard. Every year they'll get bigger and bigger and we can decorate them and they'll be beautiful!"

Weezer thumped his tail to see the look of joy that spread across the boy's face. He had no idea what Bernie was saying, but whatever it was, he liked it.

"Now all we have to do," said Mr. Jones, "is dig, let's see, ten, eleven, twelve ... twelve holes." And with that he turned to gaze at the portion of the yard where he intended to plant.

"Well I'll be," he said. "That is incredible. That is absolutely amazing. Weezer, you must be a mind-reader! Look, Bernie, he's already got the job done for us." The three of them, father, son and dog, were off across the lawn to inspect the holes, which were perfectly placed, perfectly spaced and perfect in every way.

Dreamer, who did not understand the language of humans,

watched them from across the yard, waiting for the explosion that surely must come. But something was wrong! She stood up and strained her neck to see ... the dog was not being punished! They were happy with the holes!

Dreamer twitched her tail in anger. *Humans! So unpredictable! Every single one of them! You couldn't tell from one day to the next what they would do!* She streaked across the alley to the Morton's spruce tree, where she climbed halfway up and out onto a limb. There she spent many long hours, sulking and staring off into space.

As miserable as the cat was, the dog was happy. The whole family lavished him with praise. Weezer had no idea why they were so pleased with him, but he was pretty sure it had something to do with the holes. Maybe they felt the same way he did about freshly churned up earth, its wonderful fragrance and rich dark color. Whatever their motive was, Weezer liked it, and he began planning where to place the new holes he would dig.

Later that evening Mrs. Jones decided Dreamer had had enough punishment, and she was allowed back inside before the children went to bed. She skulked into the house, had a quick bite to eat, then disappeared, just in case someone in the family was hoping to have the pleasure of a cat in their lap.

For Weezer, it had been a wonderful day. He had put in several happy hours playing Fetch! with his new ball, dining on doggie biscuits and frequently hearing his two favorite words: *"Good dog, good dog, good dog!"*

The Campout

Ever since the big boys discovered the haunted house in Peabody Gulch, Joey Wondermore had become a familiar face in the neighborhood. Though he was closer in age to the big boys, it was Bernie and Alex he gravitated toward, and the three of them were right now preparing for a campout in the Appleby's backyard.

While Bernie and Alex gathered up their stuff, Joey was in the basement of the Wondermore house, rummaging through bags and boxes, looking for his camping gear. The family had just moved to town and lots of their stuff was still packed.

Because of Mr. Wondermore's job, every three or four years the family moved to a different town. Joey hated that. It was hard to feel at home, hard to make friends. This neighborhood wasn't so bad, though; in fact, it seemed like Joey might already have a couple of friends. He didn't mind that Bernie and

Alex were two years younger. He considered them a lot more interesting than the neighborhood guys his own age.

Joey was a slender, tall boy with sandy brown hair and an inquisitive mind. A bookworm by nature, he was more of an indoor person than an outdoor person. But that was beginning to change. Since falling in league with Bernie and Alex, he had caught more garter snakes than he ever imagined he would. He waded in Peabody Creek almost every day. He climbed trees and finally learned to be accurate with a slingshot.

Before experiencing the considerable influence of Bernie and Alex, the one outdoor activity Joey had always loved was sleeping under the stars. Aha! there it was, his sleeping bag, plus his flashlight and canteen. He grabbed them and hurried toward the Appleby's yard to meet up with the other boys.

Even though it was a clear night and shelter wasn't necessary, Alex insisted they set up the Davy Crockett tent, because that made it more of an official campout. After that, there was the making of the fire, not for keeping warm, but for roasting hotdogs and marshmallows. When these tasks were accomplished, the three boys sat cross-legged on the ground, whittling their marshmallow sticks and admiring their work. It occurred to Bernie that they were a good trio; there were never any breakdowns so common to the Blazing Bandits.

"I bet we're the only kids in the whole town sleeping out tonight," said Alex. "And definitely the only ones with a campfire."

Without glancing up, the other two boys agreed.

"Everyone else is probably sitting around watching TV," Alex added.

Joey took a deep breath. "Speaking of which ... my dad's got a really nutty theory about television." He frowned as he shaved off tiny splinters with his jackknife. "He thinks it rots your brain."

Bernie and Alex exchanged astonished expressions. They had never heard of such a crazy idea. "What'dya mean it rots your brain?" asked Bernie. He imagined the gray matter in his head turning green and fuzzy with mold.

Joey heaved an enormous sigh. "He doesn't mean that it really rots your brain, it's just that when you watch TV, you begin to drift away from doing other stuff, like reading and having conversations, stuff like that. My sister and I are always trying to convince our dad that he's nuts, but our mom's part of the conspiracy, so Lisa and I are pretty much out of luck." Joey shook his head in disgust and whittled at his marshmallow stick with a vengeance. "In fact," he raised his eyes so he could watch the expressions on the other boys' faces, "we don't even own a TV."

He let that hang in the air and wondered who would be first to speak. He knew the other boys were uncomfortable and trying to think of the best thing to say. It was a scene Joey was used to. Experience had taught him to put the truth right out there so that the inevitable rejection would be easier, less embarrassing.

Bernie stopped whistling and gazed at Alex, who was and always would be incapable of disguising his emotions. His mouth was open wide, his eyes nearly popping out of his head. *Everybody had a television, even really poor people.* It was predicted that before long, color TV would become available.

"So ... if your family doesn't have a television, what do you *do* at night?" asked Bernie.

Joey whacked at the fire with his stick, regretting he'd even brought the subject up. "Well, it always takes a long time to get through dinner, on account of that my mom and dad like us to have discussions. After dinner, Lisa and I do homework, or we read. Or we all sit in the living room like a bunch of robots, listening to the radio, to some ancient old codger and his endless, totally boring music." He shrugged his shoulders, as though in apology.

Settling back against a log, Joey stabbed a marshmallow onto his stick and tried to concentrate on toasting it. He knew what to expect at this point, it had happened so many times before. Now that Bernie and Alex knew what a geeky family he had, they'd probably begin to lose interest in him, and he'd go back to being a loner again. He pictured himself as the years passed: a friendless adolescent turning into a friendless adult and finally, a friendless old man, leaning on a cane, alone and unhappy.

To himself he made the argument that he frequently made to his dad: *how many families are there that sit around and discuss books and listen to classical music?* Both he and Lisa had tried to explain that these were not normal, all-American activities; that, without a television, it was impossible to keep current with cultural trends; that being so intellectual was a huge social handicap. But, of course, their parents had refused to listen. Thus, Lisa kept to her bedroom, where she read Hollywood gossip magazines and tuned her radio to rock and roll stations. Joey frequently gazed at the intricate patterns in the wood of his bedroom wall, planning for the day he would be old enough to move away from home. He would buy the biggest TV he could find and do nothing but watch it all day, for the whole rest of his life.

Bernie, though he could not imagine life without TV, did not hold Joey's lack of one against him. He reached for another handful of potato chips and, opening his mouth wide, stuffed in as many as he could. He'd already roasted and eaten two hotdogs and, as was evident by the marshmallow goo on his face, he had eaten several of those as well. "So," Bernie said, spewing out fragments of potato chips, "you've probably read a lot of books, huh?"

"Yeah, pretty much," said Joey.

"What are your favorites?"

Surprised by the question, Joey blurted out, "Mmmm ... mostly I like to read nonfiction. I think true stories are more interesting and exciting ... but that's just my personal opinion." He hesitated to explain further. He knew he was probably alienating Bernie and Alex with this kind of talk but, thanks to his parents, he didn't know how to talk any other way.

Alex poked his stick into the fire and swished it around, sending sparks flying into the air. "You know what I like?" he said. "I like hearing stories. I'll bet you're good at telling stories, Joey. Why don't you tell us one now?"

Joey was pleased at the request. "Sure," he said, "I can tell you a story. I don't know if you'll like it, but I like it a lot. Plus, it really happened, which is a bonus, on account of that you can put yourself in other guys' shoes and try to figure out what *you'd* have done."

Bernie and Alex settled themselves more comfortably against their logs, while Joey poked two more marshmallows onto his stick. The fire crackled. Across Peabody Gulch they could hear the hoot of an owl.

"A long long time ago there lived a man named Douglas Mawson. He was a geologist, from Australia. In 1911 he went on a ship all the way down to Antarctica to study the rocks and stuff down there."

Joey inquired of the other boys, "Do you guys know that Antarctica is the coldest, windiest place in the world? It's where the South Pole is, and let me tell you, it's a whole lot colder at the South Pole than it *ever* gets at the North Pole. Also, there are lots of really tall mountains there, so when you go exploring, you have to be prepared for all kinds of stuff.

"Well this guy, Douglas Mawson, besides just gathering specimens, also wanted to see how far he could go into the interior of the continent. It was just about the only place left on the planet that people hadn't already gotten their grubby hands on. Mawson wanted to go see what was there.

"The three of them were part of a larger group of guys, all trying to accomplish certain tasks, and everyone had to meet back at their base camp by a certain day. The weather is real iffy in Antarctica, and there's not a lot of time when a ship

95

can get in or out of the ice. If any of the groups were unable to keep the rendezvous, there was no option except to leave them behind and pick them up the following year. That might sound like about the worst thing in the world, but it really wasn't, because two or three guys always volunteered to stay behind and be there for when the others came straggling in.

"So anyway, these three guys, Mawson, Mertz and Ninnis, had two sleds and two dog teams. They didn't know how long they'd be gone. They tried to figure out exactly what they would need, 'cause they had to keep their loads as light as possible and not take anything extra. But if they didn't take enough stuff and ran out of something they really needed … well that would just be too bad for them."

"How cold was it?" asked Bernie, leaning a little closer to the fire.

"Well it never got above freezing," said Joey. "With the wind chill and everything, I'd say lots of times it was, mmmmm, probably about 50 or 60 degrees below zero."

Bernie and Alex shivered reflexively, though they were not the least bit cold.

"So the three of them packed up and started out, and everything went pretty well for a while. But there are so many crevasses all over the place; you can't get away from them. Plus the wind whips the snow into these hard-packed ridges called sastrugi; some are three or four feet high. Every time they came to one that was too big to go around, they had to unpack their sleds, lift them over the ice and repack all their stuff again. They did that constantly. It was a total pain, but there was nothing they could do about it.

"But basically everything was going good. They were about 300 miles from the coast, just mushing along, happy that the weather was cooperating, when all of a sudden, the one guy, Ninnis, vanished."

Joey was a skilled storyteller and, taking off his backpack and fiddling with its elastic cord, he gave the boys time for the significance of what he had said to dawn on them.

It didn't take long. Both boys had recently seen the movie "The Blob," and they were still edgy about people who, for no obvious reason, just … disappear. Bernie looked over his right shoulder, which prompted Alex to look over his left shoulder. Though they weren't sure they wanted to know the answer, they both asked, "What happened to him?"

"Well it's a sad deal, but what happened to him is sort of a common outcome for arctic adventurers. He fell into a crevasse. It was so deep, when Mawson went to look for him, he couldn't even see all the way down to the bottom. It just went down down down, on and on forever."

As he spoke, Joey stared intently into each boy's eyes. "Along with Ninnis went all the dog food, almost all the people food, and the tent. Just like that (he snapped his fingers) the chance of the other two guys surviving and making it back to base camp on time dropped to pretty much zero."

The disaster had happened so quickly, Bernie and Alex had no idea what to say, or even what questions to ask.

"Of course, Mertz and Mawson didn't think about their own survival right away. They tried to figure out how they could possibly rescue Ninnis. They couldn't see him, but they yelled his name over and over and over, hoping he would eventually yell back. He never did though, and after a while they knew there was no chance of rescuing him." Joey stopped talking and stared into the fire.

Lost in his own thoughts, Bernie, too, stared at the flames. From the start of the story, he had imagined it was he, and Alex and Joey on the expedition. The three of them were in the icy wilderness of Antarctica, mushing dogs, collecting scientific specimens and having the grandest adventure of a lifetime. Snowy whiteness and freezing cold; Bernie could almost feel the excitement the real explorers had felt. This year for Christmas his parents had given him a new Radio Flier sled, and he loved the feeling of the wind, speeding down Peabody Hill through freshly fallen snow. He pictured himself and Alex and Joey wearing heavy jackets with fur around their hoods, trying to stand still for a photograph while their dogs jumped around, anxious to get going. But what Bernie could not picture was one of them tumbling into a canyon of ice, suddenly and forever gone. He stared hard at Alex and Joey, then gulped. *Which of the three of them would it have been?* Though it was a painful thought, it would not leave his mind.

Joey took a long sip of his Orange Nehi and said, "Well of course that was as far into the country as they went. They had a service for Ninnis, then turned around and started back for the coast. But since they had hardly any food and just a crummy little tent, which was really more like a tarp, they got really cold and hungry right away. Pretty soon they ran out of food altogether."

"So what did they eat?" asked Alex.

Joey sucked in his cheeks and said a thing that was hard for him to say. "They had to eat the dogs."

"No!" said Bernie, refusing to believe it was true.

"They had to," said Joey. "They were starving. If they hadn't, they would've died."

A big part of Bernie's fantasy was imagining a dog team composed of the neighborhood dogs, including Weezer, Streak, the Wolverton's terrier, and Mr. Cunningham's chihuahua, King George.

"They ate the dogs?"

"That might sound pretty bad to you," said Joey, "but when you're tromping around in the Antarctic and it's a matter of life or death, you do what you have to.

"Whatever else they had for rations, they carefully divided. Each man got about, mmm, half a cup of food to last him all day.

"They hadn't gone far when Mertz started to get sick. He just kept getting worse and worse. After a while he was so weak, he couldn't walk anymore. That meant when the weather was okay and they could make some progress, Mawson would put Mertz in the sled and pull him.

"Their progress dropped to almost nothing. It started to look less and less like they would make it."

Joey, who loved gazing at fires, stared at the one in front of him and pondered the endurance of the great man, Douglas Mawson. First and foremost, he was a scientist. Even after the disaster of losing a man, and the sudden, severe illness of the other, Mawson never considered discarding the geological specimens he'd been collecting; it was, after all, the purpose of the trip. Most likely, Mawson knew that Mertz was doomed, that he himself had little hope of survival. Joey, as he had many times, wondered what had been on Mawson's mind as he pulled his sick companion mile after endless mile.

Bernie waited for Joey to resume his tale, though as much as he wanted to know what happened next, he wanted to turn away from the knowing of it. He wanted to go back to roasting marshmallows and having fun, telling jokes. All his life, whenever Bernie heard stories or references to suffering, it had a powerful effect on him, so that it was hard to go back to whatever he'd been doing. Totally captive to the experiences of men he would never meet, Bernie looked over his shoulder toward the Davy Crockett tent, wiped away a tear and prepared himself to hear the bad news about Mawson and Mertz.

"They made it pretty far. They were about a hundred miles from their destination, but then the weather got real bad. They were in a storm so wild, they couldn't see even a few feet ahead of them. They had to stay in their tent for days and days. Mertz kept getting worse. Finally he died."

The three boys stared into the fire, not daring to look at one another.

As he had previously, when he got to this part of the story, Joey grew silent. He couldn't help wracking his brain, determined to make sense of this tragedy, to see it for more than it was on the surface.

So much time passed, finally he said, "There were just ... so many crevasses. Mawson was in so much danger. Really, there was no reason for him to think he would survive. But he was a really determined kind of guy. Stubborn. There was no way in the world he was going to just sit there and wait to freeze to death. He had a funeral service for Mertz, then he put his supplies on his sled and he kept on going.

"His body was wasting away from lack of nutrients and all the hardships he had to deal with. His hands were so badly damaged from freezing and thawing, they were just useless stubs. His feet started giving him problems. His heels began to separate from his feet; he had to wrap them with rags to keep them from coming off altogether. But he kept on going. He was a guy with a lot of guts.

"One day he fell into a crevasse. He came real close to getting killed, but it gave him an idea: to make a rope ladder and attach it to his sled. If he fell into a another hole, the sled might anchor him, and he could climb out. His idea worked; three or four times he'd have been a goner if he hadn't come up with that.

"He was so weak and in such bad shape, it took him about three hours each evening to set up his tent. You can imagine how hard it was for him to light his little camp stove. He boiled dog bones into a mushy glop; it was his only food. He fell into so many crevasses, he stopped counting them, but with his rope ladder, he was able to get out of every one.

"Finally one day he saw something, a flag sticking up out of the snow. Men from the other expeditions had been looking for the three explorers, Mawson, Ninnis and Mertz. Their boat had to get going or it would become stuck in the ice, so they'd gone out looking for Mawson and his men several times. They went as far as they could, then built a kind of a fort and loaded it up with food and a little stove to make a fire. They left a note too. When Mawson found it, he knew he would survive." Joey shook his head in disbelief. "It was an incredible coincidence that Mawson found that flag and the fort. I bet the chances were, oh I'd say, about a jillion to one."

Bernie almost wept with joy. He rubbed his hands and held them closer to the fire. He made eye contact with Alex and they exchanged smiles of relief.

Joey took a deep breath. "That's the story of Douglas Mawson. When my grandpa was fourteen, he met him one time when Mawson was on a tour of the United States. It was at a museum in Chicago. He got his autograph. He got to shake his hand, too." Joey held out his right hand for Bernie and Alex to admire. "This is the hand that shook the hand of the man who touched Douglas Mawson."

Both boys instinctively leaned forward to touch Joey's hand.

The fire had burned down to a nice bed of coals. Joey, who had only eaten one hotdog, was ready for a s'more. He reached for a marshmallow, poked it onto the end of a willow stick and held it over the coals.

A strange sensation washed over Bernie. He reached for a marshmallow, then thought of the hunger Mawson had suffered and stuffed his hand into his pocket instead. He was chilly, too, now that the fire had burned low, but he didn't put on his jacket. He just shivered and stared off into the starry night. He was thinking about what Joey had said, wondering about jillion-to-one coincidences.

A jillion to one. Hmmmm. Bernie's thoughts wandered to a disturbing idea that had lately planted itself in his mind. It started with something he had seen on TV a while back, on the evening news. During an interview, the Russian leader, Khrushchev, had angrily banged his fist and promised he would bury all the Americans, meaning he just might drop some atom bombs and kill everyone if he felt like it. The thought of it terrified Bernie, but such a thing really could happen. In school, they sometimes prepared for it by hiding under their desks and covering their faces with their hands. Very soon, like many other people in town, Bernie's father would begin digging a bomb shelter. As much as it sounded like living in a bomb shelter could be sort of fun, if Bernie thought about it very much, he usually ended up with a stomach ache

If the world really were so unpredictable that bombs could destroy everything, then there might also be *other* things, equally bad things. Like the blob. A guy could just be minding his own business and, all of a sudden, the blob might roll into his yard and gobble him up. Or a spaceship could land in your back yard and take you off to another planet. Or you could be exploring in Antarctica, and suddenly you're the only guy alive, and just when you think your luck has totally run out, you see a flag sticking up out of a snow bank. *The world was such a big place. Anything, really, could happen.*

"Well, I'm heading for the tent," said Alex. "I've got my flashlight and a couple new comics. I'll share 'em with you when you come in." He took a few steps toward the tent, yawned with gusto, then turned around and said, "That was a great story, Joey. I'm sure glad you decided to come camping with us."

"*You are?*" said Joey. He was genuinely surprised. Most kids, when they got to know him even a little, thought he was too ... something. Too smart, maybe. Too different from how they were. It felt great to be accepted.

Joey finished his s'more and said, "Yeah, well I think I'll turn in too. How about you, Bern? Ready to call it a day?"

"Mmm, not quite," said Bernie. "I think I'll just sit here for a few more minutes." Then there was silence, and Bernie was left alone. He worked the tip of his hotdog stick back and forth, back and forth, in the few remaining embers, staring blankly, thinking a hundred things at once and not really thinking about anything at all. It was funny how you could be so sure something was going to be a certain way, and then it turned out not to be that way at all. He had been looking forward to this camping trip all week, ever since Alex had suggested it on Monday. Bernie figured they'd sit around and tell ghost stories and jokes and relive old adventures. Probably there'd be lots of laughs.

But it hadn't turned out that way at all. It was still fun, and he was glad to be camping, but it wasn't fun in the usual laughter-and-jokes kind of way. Bernie whacked his hotdog stick against the rocks that framed the fire pit - tap tap tap tap - his mind reeling. He kept thinking about Douglas Mawson and his terrible ordeal. He couldn't erase the picture from his mind: one man, all alone, trudging through the Antarctic wilderness. A guy who had lost everything, whose life was in danger with every step he took. An hour ago, Bernie hadn't even heard of Douglas Mawson; now he felt huge, real feelings for him and his jillion-to-one survival.

What that had to do with the blob or the Russians, Bernie did not know. He just knew that they were connected, somehow. With the highlights of Joey's story playing again and again through his mind, with the twinkling of stars overhead and the soft hooting of a nearby owl, Bernie felt something crack, way down deep inside himself, the way the earth cracks, to form crevasses in places far far away.

The Fishing Trip

The first rays of light began to appear in the eastern sky as Bernie Jones hurried out his front door. He had his lunch in a sack and his fishing pole in his hand. He was going to the senior center to meet up with Grandpa.

There was something about early morning that, to Bernie, was extra special. As he crossed the alley to Park Street, he took in deep breaths of chilly air and shivered into the warmth of his jacket. There were hardly any cars, and the few lights that shined in the houses seemed to glow.

Though it was still more dark than light, Bernie was not afraid. This was his neighborhood. He knew everyone and everyone knew him. Across the street he saw the Murphy's big black and white cat sitting on their front porch, licking his paws. Three houses beyond Murphy's, Bernie could see old

Mrs. Wolverton opening her door, stepping outside, carefully making her way down her steps. She wore a pink sweater and leaned on her cane. Having observed her for many years, Bernie knew she would now walk two blocks down Park Street and, despite the absence of any cars, wait at the crossing until the light turned green, trot across the street and walk home on the other side.

Good old Mrs. Wolverton. She had the biggest lilac tree in the neighborhood and always welcomed everyone to cut bouquets from it. After her morning walk, before she went inside, she would stand for a minute or two to gaze at her tree and breathe in its strong sweet smell.

Then Bernie was beyond Mrs. Wolverton. Already a much bigger chunk of the sky was getting lighter. Down the street he could see the senior center. Grandpa would be waiting near the side door, with his pole and his bait and his bucket.

There he was, all ready to go. But this morning, unlike all the times before, his friend Mr. Jenkins was with him. As the two elderly gentlemen hurried down the walkway, away from the senior center, they frequently looked over their shoulders, acting suspiciously.

"Shhh," whispered Grandpa, when Bernie opened his mouth to ask what was going on. "Mrs. Bukovinic just came on duty. If she sees us sneaking out, she'll be on us like fleas on a hound."

Mrs. Bukovinic was the head nurse. She took her job seriously and often came across as quite stern. She felt it was crucial that all the nurses obey every rule in the big book of rules.

The book was kept at the nurses' station, where it could easily be referred to. As Grandpa had pointed out, and Bernie knew just by watching, most people were afraid of Mrs. Bukovinic. She knew it too, but she didn't care much.

Though there was no rule about it, Mrs. Bukovinic seemed to think that early morning was not the proper time to be any too cheerful. A smile was all right, but joking and laughter were discouraged, either by a quick scowl, or a comment referring to the fact that a job as serious as nursing requires a serious attitude.

Mrs. Bukovinic drank several cups of coffee each morning. By the time she was on her fourth or fifth cup, her sense of humor usually returned, and she became the pleasant, cheerful person she generally was. The other nurses were familiar with the ups and downs of her temperament and usually waited until her coffee cup was pushed aside before approaching her with anything challenging.

When the three of them were beyond the senior center, Grandpa said to Bernie, "Hope you don't mind if I bring along my partner. Fred hasn't been fishing in a long time." He then added in a much louder voice, "Have you, Fred?"

"What's that?" said Mr. Jenkins, cupping his hand around his ear.

Grandpa all but shouted, "I said, it's been too long since you've been fishing."

"Sure enough," said Mr. Jenkins, which is how he always responded when he didn't quite hear what was being said.

Grandpa and Mr. Jenkins had been a pinochle-playing team for many years. Almost every day they sat in the parlor of the senior center and played cards with other pairs of old folks. Rarely did they lose.

Down Park Street the three of them walked, Grandpa and Bernie side by side and Mr. Jenkins in front. Over the years Bernie had gotten to know Mr. Jenkins pretty well. He was a skinny, shrunken man, kind of hunched over, with a head of white hair and thick, horn-rimmed glasses. He always wore a plaid flannel shirt, gray pants and a baseball cap. His hearing used to be a whole lot better, and he used to move a lot faster. Bernie took a long look at him and noticed, for the first time, that Mr. Jenkins was starting to look really old.

Grandpa put his arm around Bernie's shoulder and said, "This is probably Fred's last fishing trip."

"Is he going somewhere?" Bernie asked.

Grandpa shrugged. "I don't know. Could be."

"He's been your partner for a long time, huh?" said Bernie.

"Sure has," Grandpa answered. "I'm gonna miss him."

Bernie was just getting ready to ask why Grandpa would miss Mr. Jenkins, when he wasn't going anywhere, but then two things happened at once. All the street lights blinked off, as they did this time each morning, leaving the street momentarily in twilight. Then, on the horizon, Bernie could see the first golden rays of the sun.

As if they had earlier agreed to do so, the three fishermen stopped and stared at the beauty of the sunrise. They all breathed deeply, inhaling the sweet smell of flowers and the salt water breeze drifting in from the sea. Each of them, for his own private reasons, was ever so grateful to be going fishing.

When they got to the harbor, they picked their way through the stone breakwater to the fishing beach. The closer they got to the shore, the more Mr. Jenkins seemed to liven his pace.

Grandpa had two buckets filled with tackle and gear stacked inside each other. Mr. Jenkins, though he hadn't been fishing in a long time, was the first to bait his hook and toss it into the chilly water. Bernie noticed how knobby and gnarled his hands were, recalling that Mr. Jenkins had once been a skilled jeweler. His business had relied on the nimbleness of his fingers.

Grandpa would have brought along a bucket for Bernie, too, but there was no way could Bernie sit down; that wasn't his style. He liked to wander along the beach, making a few casts here and a few casts there. He couldn't say exactly what it was about the spots that he chose; mostly it was just a lucky feeling that would suddenly overtake him. He would make a silent wish for fish, then cast out his line.

He knew he'd stand more of a chance of catching something if he stayed in one spot but, as Grandpa always said, there's a lot more to fishing than just catching fish. With these words of wisdom, Bernie meandered at will, relying on his intuition for guidance.

After an hour or so, Grandpa caught the first one, a nice fat cod, nearly twelve inches long. He caught another one soon thereafter, and then Mr. Jenkins was reeling in his line with a look of amazement on his face; he too had caught a fish, the biggest so far. As he pulled it onto the shore, he moved like a much younger man, bending easily, feeling sure of himself. He commented once to Grandpa, once to Bernie and once to a stranger who happened to be fishing in the same spot, that it was such a good-looking fish, he almost hated to catch it.

Bernie didn't have the luck - or perhaps it was the skill - of the older men, and after an hour or so he decided to take a break, eat one of his sandwiches and go for a walk. As he wandered away from Grandpa and Mr. Jenkins, he imagined that he was the first person ever to be here, in this exact spot. He quickly put a story together in his mind and became the single survivor of a shipwreck, with this stretch of beach for his front yard. Years earlier, when he first washed ashore, he had built a sturdy tree house. With Peabody Creek nearby, there was plenty of fresh water, and his food was swimming nearby.

As Bernie continued down the beach, he picked up a long stick and wrote his name in the sand. He drew a hopscotch and played with it a while. Then he dragged the stick down the beach, making curlicues and flipping rocks and seaweed into the air. A curious beachcomber, Bernie constantly turned over shells, upended smaller logs and poked his stick into piles of whatever the sea had seen fit to deliver to the shore.

Suddenly he found it, the thing he had always heard about but never imagined

112

he would be lucky enough to find: a bottle ... with a message inside! It was an old-fashioned bottle, small and fancy, with glass so thick it was hard to see through. When he held it up to the light, he could see, there was definitely a rolled up piece of paper inside. He waved it high above his head and shouted, "Grandpa! Grandpa! Look what I found!"

His voice carried on the morning breeze, so jubilant and excited, even Mr. Jenkins heard him loud and clear. He turned to see his friend's grandson racing down the beach with a grin a mile wide.

"Look," Bernie shouted, holding out the bottle. "It's got a message inside!"

Mr. Jenkins couldn't hear the rest; the boy was too excited; his words came out too fast. But he could see the object in his hand, so Mr. Jenkins reeled in his line and walked down the beach toward Bernie.

Mr. Jenkins was grateful that he'd been included today. He hadn't been out of the senior center in weeks, since Mrs. Bukovinic had informed him and his son and daughter-in-law that from now on, Mr. Jenkins would have to use a wheelchair if he left the building. The younger people took the news as though it wasn't any big thing, just one more detail that Mr. Jenkins would have to work his way around. To Mr. Jenkins, it was a huge blow. After they had left, he wished he had scolded the young people who now had such control over his life. Sometimes, though it made no sense, he even blamed them that he was getting so old.

Since there was no use trying to explain his feelings to the younger generation, Mr. Jenkins later walked down to Gus Jones's room and told him the whole story. Grandpa immediately understood what his friend was saying. Several times during the telling of Mr. Jenkins' story, Grandpa shook his head with sorrow and anger, though there was no one to be angry with.

"Gol darn it," Grandpa said, his eyes never leaving Mr. Jenkins' face. He wanted his old friend to know that, not only did he understand what was being said; he understood how Mr. Jenkins felt. Grandpa hadn't driven for years, but that wasn't the point. The point was the inability of Mr. Jenkins to control his own life. So, naturally, he was thrilled when Gus Jones proposed that they more or less sneak out of the senior center to go fishing. Right now the lifelong law-abiding Mr. Jenkins didn't give a diddly darn for the rules.

When he reached the spot where the other two were, he could see what all the commotion was about. The bottle that the boy had been waving around had a message inside. It wasn't any too easy to get open, though, as it was plugged with a thick cork.

With his pliers, Grandpa was working on the cork, carefully wiggling it this way and that. In his excitement, Bernie danced around, trying to get a closer look. He couldn't wait to read the note.

In the next moment, the cork was off and Grandpa was handing the bottle to Bernie, whose hands shook with the thrill of discovery. Is there anything so wonderful to an explorer as finding a message in a bottle?

It took some maneuvering to get the paper out, but when he did, Bernie's jaw dropped in surprise. The note had only eight words: "Help! I am stuck on a deserted island."

Grandpa read the note, Mr. Jenkins read the note, and they exchanged skeptical looks. They didn't think it was for real.

"Wha'd'ya mean it's not for real?" said Bernie. "Sure it is. It's from a guy who's stuck on a deserted island. It's our responsibility to find some way to help him."

"Well now, Bernie, maybe it is and maybe it isn't," said Grandpa, who was starting to get a little tired and had noticed some fatigue in the eyes of Mr. Jenkins. "Wouldn't you figure that a guy who needed rescuing would give you some instructions about how to find him?"

"Maybe he doesn't know where he is," said Bernie.

Mr. Jenkins, who had to shout in order to hear himself, hollered, "Could be that this is someone's idea of a practical joke."

Bernie examined the note some more while Mr. Jenkins scrutinized the bottle, which was dark green and irregular in shape. He turned it over and over in his hands, holding it up to the light. Then he brought it to his lips, held it just so and blew out a deep, beautiful note. What a sound! Like a musical instrument! It pleased him so much, he blew on the bottle again and again before handing it back. He waited until Bernie coaxed out the same soothing sound, then Mr. Jenkins wandered back down the beach, cast out his line and went back to fishing.

Grandpa baited his hook and said to Bernie, "Before we get too excited and call out the state militia, let's both think about this some more." He too went back to fishing.

The bottle in one hand and the note in the other, Bernie stood on the beach and studied the graceful handwriting, wondering who could have written it? Were they really in trouble? How could he help?

He put the note back inside the bottle, then set it down on the sand by his fishing gear. He cast out his line a few more times, but his heart wasn't on the task. Had the writer of the message been shipwrecked? How long ago? Later, he would show the note to his parents, and on Monday he'd show it to Miss Jamison. She was good at solving mysteries; she would know how to go about getting help.

They would find the stranded person and hear all about his adventures. Even if it turned out that it *was* a hoax, it was still an extra-special thing, that the bottle had floated here, to this exact beach, and that he, Bernie Jones, had found it.

Bernie was vaguely aware that Grandpa had caught another fish, and Mr. Jenkins had reeled in another one too. But when he looked up from his daydreaming, he could see that something was wrong with Mr. Jenkins. Bernie ran to find out what it was.

"He's short of breath," said Grandpa, trying not to sound panicked. "We've gotta get him back to the senior center right away. Here." He dug in his pocket for some change. "Go call your dad and tell him to come and pick us up."

Bernie took off as fast as he could run. Five minutes later his dad arrived and helped the two old men into the car.

"But I'm not ready to go back yet," Mr. Jenkins protested. "I only caught two fish, and besides, I feel fine."

"Well you don't look so fine," said Grandpa. "And as for fishing ... we'll come another day."

Bernie's dad put the car in gear and headed back up the street. He knew to park by the side door at the senior center and not to make a sound when he helped his father and Mr. Jenkins inside.

When they got to the door, Grandpa tried to warn Mr. Jenkins that he should keep his voice down. But his friend didn't hear the warning, plus he wanted to complain some more about not having had enough time to fish. The result was that Mrs. Bukovinic heard the commotion and came clomp clomp clomping from the nurse's station to the side door, wearing her sparkling white uniform, starched white cap and an extra-large scowl on her face.

"And just where have you two been?" she asked, even though it was perfectly obvious.

"We caught some nice codfish this morning, Vivian," Grandpa said, reaching into the top bucket and holding up a fine, fat specimen. "You know, you've gotta be there at sunup if you want to catch fish. We didn't want to disturb anyone, so we took the side door."

"Mmm hmm," she said, tapping her foot and frowning at Grandpa.

"A beautiful cod like this would make a wonderful dinner," Grandpa continued. He sweetened his tone a bit. "It'd cost you a fortune if you bought it in the supermarket." He held it out to her. "But today, for you, it's free."

Mrs. Bukovinic's frown seemed to loosen up a little, and she looked the fish over with interest. Grandpa winked at his son.

"Well we've gotta go now," said Bernie's dad. "Good luck," he whispered to his father, as he and Bernie headed for the door.

As soon as they got in the car, Bernie quickly explained about the bottle, and the two of them examined it, along with the note.

"Do you think we should take it to the police?" said Bernie.

"Or maybe the Coast Guard?"

Seeing as how his dad was remaining quiet on the matter, Bernie let his gaze rest on the water and the mountains across the bay. "I know what to do," he said. "On Monday I'll take it to school and show it to Miss Jamison. She'll have a good idea. She always knows what to do." The gears in Bernie's brain were grinding out a scenario in which he was included in the rescue team. Miss Jamison would be too. It would make headlines all over the world. The thought of such an adventure made Bernie positively glow.

Just then they passed Mrs. Wolverton, out in her yard, clipping a bouquet of lilacs. She smiled and waved.

Good old Mrs. Wolverton, thought Bernie. After he'd had a bit of breakfast, he'd walk over to her house; she'd be interested to see the bottle and the note. And of course, he'd show it to Alex right away. And Clark Olsen, too. If Clark was at all impressed with it, maybe Bernie and Alex would be allowed to attend meetings of the Blazing Bandits again.

For the first time that day, Bernie realized he was wearing his lucky shirt, which didn't surprise him at all, considering what kind of day it had been. First there was the sunrise, and going fishing and finding the bottle. Now he could dazzle everyone with his treasure, and maybe he could be one of the rescuers and hear first-hand how the writer of the note came to be stranded on a deserted island. He might even get his picture in the newspaper.

Bernie felt the warm sun on his face and the sweet anticipation of the day ahead. Life was so exciting, and he was right in the middle of living it. Which is why it surprised him to hear his dad say, "Too bad you didn't catch anything." Bernie answered without hesitation. "You know Dad, there's a lot more to fishing than just catching fish."

The Birthday Party

The last thing in the whole world the Patterson twins wanted on their fourteenth birthday was to invite Bernie Jones and Alex Appleby to their party. But, thanks to Mrs. Patterson, Bernie and Alex *were* invited, and nothing could be done about it now.

A few days before the big event, Mrs. Patterson ran into Mrs. Jones in the cereal aisle of Shop and Save. In the process of neighborly chitchat, Mrs. Patterson mentioned her sons' upcoming party: what a festive occasion it would be, that all the neighborhood boys were invited, there'd be hours of fun, including basketball and miniature golf and darts. There was even a seven-layer birthday cake, which Mrs. Patterson described as "a chocolate lover's dream."

"Gosh," said Mrs. Jones. "This is the first time I've heard about the twins' birthday party. Are you sure Bernie and Alex are invited?"

The cheeks of the always-polite Mrs. Patterson turned a deep shade of scarlet and, too stunned to answer the question, she began planning the lecture she would give the twins when she returned from the grocery.

Noting Mrs. Patterson's embarrassment, Mrs. Jones was quick to assure her, "Oh don't worry about it, Charlotte. After all, Bernie and Alex are four years younger; it's understandable that Richard and Robert wouldn't want to include them. Don't give it a moment's thought." In her heart of hearts, however, she knew Bernie and Alex would be disappointed.

"No no no no no," Mrs. Patterson insisted. "The invitation must have gotten lost in the mail. I know my boys planned to include them. We've all been neighbors forever. Why, I re-member Bernie toddling around in diapers." She glanced at her list, "Well I've got to go. Toodle-oo," she said, wiggling her fingers at Mrs. Jones. "And don't forget about Saturday. I'll tell Robert and Richard to give the boys a call so there won't be any more confusion."

Mrs. Jones studied the brightly colored boxes of cereal much longer than necessary, considering she wasn't planning to buy cereal. What an odd encounter with her neighbor. Oh well, she decided, the boys could either go to the party or not go; it was their choice. There were too many ups and downs in family life to take things like this very seriously. Later, when she happened into a clothing store and saw a two-for-one sale on Superman T-shirts (currently all the rage among the teen-age set) she couldn't resist the urge to buy a pair, just in case a gift-giving occasion arose.

✳✳✳✳✳✳✳✳✳✳

At that precise moment the Blazing Bandits - minus Bernie and Alex - were holding an emergency meeting in the old abandoned shack in Mr. Cornelius's apple orchard. The five boys sat in a semicircle, their attention more or less focused on Clark Olsen.

"The meeting is now called to order," said Clark, pounding a wooden gavel against the side of the clubhouse. "Now listen up, men. We've gotta decide: do we want to keep Bernie Jones and Alex Appleby in the Bandits, or don't we?"

There was no response. Clark busied himself picking at a hangnail, telling himself what he should do was leave it alone entirely. Fiddling with hangnails always made them worse.

The Patterson twins were, as usual, scuffling around, trying to keep their shenanigans to a minimum and still manage to maul one another to the greatest degree. Brian Shaunessey was deeply engrossed in a Spider Man comic book. Larry Rustalio was attempting to invisibly reach into his lunch sack for the remainder of his dessert.

Frustrated by the endless foolings around of the Patterson twins, Clark ripped his hangnail till it caused a piercing pain in his fingertip. This made him so mad, he banged the gavel even harder against the wall. "Quiet down you bums! Show some respect! Geez!" He gave them each a mean, threatening look and shook his head at their worthlessness.

Richard and Robert quickly grew straight-faced but, as everyone knew, they were only pretending, for they were already digging their elbows into each other's ribs. Larry Rustalio was glad the attention was momentarily on someone else, as he quickly reached into his lunch bag for the chocolate cream puff he had been saving. Large and growing larger every day, Larry was still nimble as a cat. To protect his food, he could run, dodge, roll and duck and rarely lose a morsel.

Though he was unaware of it, Brian Shaunessey was learning a lesson that would come in handy when he got to college: how to read in the midst of chaos. Even with the twins goofing around and Clark banging the gavel and shouting for order, Brian never lost his place in whatever comic book he happened to be reading. Though none of the Bandits would admit it, their meetings were pretty much a complete waste of time.

The comic books were probably the most outstanding thing about their club. The very best of each boy's collection had been saved over the years. They were kept in the clubhouse in wooden boxes and treated in a remarkably respectful fashion, considering the antics that took place in the shack.

Clark pulled a comb from his back pocket and slid it through his hair in the style of Elvis Presley. "Sooner or later word is bound to leak out about us having a couple of ten-year-olds in our club. It's gonna make us look pretty bad. Guys in other clubs will make fun of us. Is that something we want?"

Brian Shaunessey looked up from his Spider Man comic and opened his mouth to speak in Bernie and Alex's defense, but Clark cut him off. "I know, I know, I know. Bernie Jones can eat two quarts of mayonnaise."

Brian attempted to speak again, but Clark interjected, "Yeah, and I know Alex Appleby's parents own the Lincoln Theater, which *could* come in handy some day."

Larry Rustalio, his last bite of chocolate cream puff oozing out the sides of his mouth, said, "Yeah, whatever happened to those free movie passes you promised us, Clark? You said if we let Bernie and Alex in the club, we'd all get free movie passes. Popcorn too." All the other Bandits agreed and waited to hear what Clark had to say.

Clark frowned and smacked the gavel into the palm of his hand. This was a crucial moment; he was in danger of looking foolish. He had to choose his words carefully. *Think!* he told himself. *Think!*

"Look at it this way." Clark stared at each boy individually in an intense, scrutinizing way. "This Saturday afternoon the twins are having a huge birthday party. We're talking major food here, barbecued burgers, hotdogs, potato salad, the works. And I'm pretty sure - he leaned in and spoke in a loud whisper - there'll be some junior high girls stopping by."

"*Girls?*" Brian said.

Clark nodded. "So," he continued, "you get the picture. We're all having fun and then along come our good buddies, the other two members of our club, a couple of ten-year-olds."

Brian Shaunessey was instantly vexed. He wanted to do the right thing, to defend Bernie and Alex but, more and more, girls had begun to occupy his mind. Clark Olsen had been girl-crazy for years. Even Larry Rustalio had a certain girl he occasionally walked with between classes.

Though Clark had no reason to think any girls might truly come to the party, just the thought of it was enough to convince the other boys it was time to drop Bernie and Alex from the Blazing Bandits.

✳✳✳✳✳✳✳✳✳✳

When her shopping trip ended and Mrs. Patterson had successfully wedged her big Oldsmobile into the garage, she wasted no time in beckoning Richard and Robert to the kitchen. There she informed them that Alex Appleby and Bernie Jones were absolutely to be invited to the birthday party.

"That's not fair," Richard, the elder of the two, insisted, stamping his foot so hard the china figurines on the kitchen window sill wobbled back and forth. "It's our party, and we don't want any little kids!"

"Yeah!" said Robert, who normally went out of his way to disagree with his brother. "It's our party, and we don't want any little kids."

"Well boys, I'll give you a choice," said Mrs. Patterson, who was big on choices. "Either you have a party which includes Bernie and Alex, or you have no party at all. Now, which will it be?"

✳✳✳✳✳✳✳✳✳✳

Unaware of what was happening at the Patterson house, Clark Olsen shouted the bad news over the back yard fence to Bernie and Alex as they lay sprawled on the Appleby's lawn. Being voted out of the Blazing Bandits was a disappointment for the two of them, but it wasn't a surprise. At first, after their initiation, they had been included in all the secret doings of the Bandits. Lately, though, the older boys had begun ignoring them publicly, holding meetings without telling them and generally treating them with scorn.

✳✳✳✳✳✳✳✳✳

Alex was confused when he received the birthday invitation from Richard Patterson and ran straight to the Jones's house, where Bernie was just getting off the phone with Robert Patterson. "Wow!" said Alex, his face glowing with happiness, "Maybe this means they're going to ask us to join the Bandits again." He pushed his thick eyeglasses back into place and smiled a toothy, hopeful grin.

"Maybe," said Bernie, because even though being invited to a birthday party was usually a lucky thing, in this particular case he had a feeling that what it meant was trouble.

✳✳✳✳✳✳✳✳✳

When Mrs. Jones returned from her shopping trip, in addition to all her bags of groceries, she had two other bags as well. One contained the two Superman T-shirts. The other contained enough underwear to see Bernie through the rest of the school year.

Later on that night, when she was wrapping the birthday gifts, the two bags got mixed up, and instead of giving the twins each a Superman T-shirt, she wrapped a three-pack of jockey shorts for each of them. She hummed along with the radio as she carefully curled the ribbon of each package, pleased that the Superman T-shirts were something the older boys would be truly thrilled to receive.

✳✳✳✳✳✳✳✳✳

The day of the birthday party dawned bright and beautiful. Alex and his mother spent most of the day shopping for birthday gifts, while Bernie did chores and homework. At precisely 3:55 p.m., the two boys headed down the street toward the Patterson's house.

Despite their protests, both boys were freshly bathed and wearing clean shirts, and their hair was combed. Alex's hair was the agreeable kind that lays down flat and doesn't pop back up and look weird. But Bernie had the sort of hair that, especially when it was squeaky clean, gave him lots of trouble. There was one hunk of it, right in front, that always stuck out at an odd angle. The only way to keep it in place was to put lots of Brylcream on it and comb it down about a thousand times. Today, to make sure it behaved, Bernie put a whole lot of extra Brylcream on it and combed it about two thousand times, until his hand started to hurt.

Unlike the ten-year-olds, all the big boys understood that guests don't arrive at parties precisely the moment they are supposed to begin. So, of course, Bernie and Alex were the first ones to arrive.

It was an outdoor party, and the Pattersons' dart board, which was normally kept in the basement, was now fixed to the side of the house. As Bernie and Alex approached, Richard and

Robert argued about whose turn it was, and who had won the last game, and who was the better player.

"Yoo hoo!" Mrs. Patterson shouted from the kitchen window, when she saw Bernie and Alex. "Glad you boys could make it!"

In a singsong voice Richard said, "Yeah, glad you boys could make it!" Not to be outdone, Robert repeated, "Yeah, glad you boys could make it."

This was standard behavior for the Patterson boys, so Alex didn't take offense at their tone. At that precise moment, Bernie suddenly had to deal with Weezer, who had been following at a distance and now refused to go home.

"Hey! Who said you could bring your dog to our birthday party?" Richard asked Bernie. "If he chases my cat, I'm telling you right now, I'll throw a rock at him."

Just about that time, all the other big boys showed up: Clark Olsen, Brian Shaunessey and Larry Rustalio. As they approached the house, Clark Olsen withdrew his comb from his back pocket and slicked it through his hair a few times. The three of them were hoping against hope that maybe a few of the older neighborhood girls would show up. In particular,

Clark was wishing for a glimpse of Lisa Wondermore.

The boys had been forewarned, of course, that Bernie and Alex would be at the party, but since they were out of the club now, this wasn't of any particular concern.

As Clark neared the Patterson house, he took one look at Bernie and laughed out loud. "Hey Beanbrain," he said, pointing at Bernie's hair, "it looks like you could use a comb." He held out his own comb, meaning to pull it back just at the right moment, to make Bernie look even more foolish.

But just then Mrs. Patterson poked her head out the kitchen window and hollered hello to the three older boys, at which time, Bernie took Clark's comb and ran it through the unruly front of his hair. When he handed it back, it was oozing with Brylcream.

"Yuck!" said Clark, making a big show of flicking the greasy white stuff onto the lawn. Since it was their birthday and they could get away with it, Richard and Robert laughed out loud at Clark and mimicked the troubles with his comb. This got Brian and Larry laughing, too, for they rarely had a chance to make Clark look like a fool without paying for it somehow. Clark Olsen was one of those guys who took himself so seriously, most of the time you didn't dare laugh at him.

Bernie didn't notice Clark's scorn, because Alex was handing him three darts and challenging him to a game, and at last the fun was beginning.

Eventually the big boys were so absorbed in their own game of basketball, they failed to notice ... Bernie Jones was an excellent dart thrower. Unlike Alex, who could barely manage to even hit the board, Bernie was throwing bulls eyes every third or fourth try. When one of the boys finally did notice, they all crowded around and, except for Clark, congratulated Bernie on his skill and challenged him to game after game. Bernie beamed with pride. Not only was he beating all the big boys at darts, he had overheard Brian telling Clark that maybe they should let him back in the Blazing Bandits. "Even though he's only ten years old," Brian had said, "he's got a lot of talent."

The boys ate hamburgers and hotdogs and potato salad, and just when they thought they couldn't eat another bite, Mrs. Rustalio showed up with her famous seven-layer chocolate birthday cake, and all the 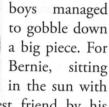 boys managed to gobble down a big piece. For Bernie, sitting in the sun with his best friend by his side, and the thought that maybe they would again be allowed to join the Blazing Bandits, this day was almost too good to be true.

And of course, it was too good to be true.

The minute the dessert was eaten, Richard and Robert dove for their pile of gifts. Both

132

of them had grass in their hair from their earlier scuffle and twice they had interrupted the basketball game to torment each other. But now, with their mother standing by, a camera in her hand, and all the presents yet to be opened, they became model citizens.

"Thank you," they politely told Clark, when each of them had opened his gift of baseball cards.

"Thank you," they told Brian, for the multicolored frisbees.

"Thank you," they told Larry, for the twin transistor radios, which, unfortunately, did not have batteries, and never would, since they were both destroyed before the party was over.

They were also polite to Alex for the model cars, even though there was a brief scuffle over who got the Corvette and who got the Thunderbird.

Bernie's gift was the last they opened. As their mother stood poised to snap another picture, Richard and Robert ripped off the paper, tore into the boxes and discovered that they each had three new pairs of underwear.

It's hard to say whose face turned reddest: Richard's or Robert's or Bernie's.

Mrs. Patterson, who prided herself on always knowing how to behave in any social situation, immediately thought of something nice to say: "How sweet! Bernie has given you boys a *practical* gift!"

From the looks on Richard and Robert's faces, Bernie knew

he better say the right thing, and say it quick, because otherwise he and Alex would never make it back into the Blazing Bandits. But when he opened his mouth, instead of telling the twins it was all a big mistake and that their real gifts were Superman T-shirts, what came out was, "Hey, that's *my* underwear!"

Which made things worse. Robert immediately dropped his gift, as though it had cooties. Richard, because he was so embarrassed to be standing there in front of all the other teenagers with three pairs of jockey shorts in his hand, did the first thing he thought of, pulled out one pair and fitted it over his brother's head. It sort of looked like a chef's hat. Not to be outdone, Robert hooked a pair over Richard's head, which made every boy in the yard laugh so hard and so long, they all felt weak.

As luck would have it, right at that moment, the oldest Baxter girl, Elizabeth, along with her friend Cindy - both fourteen years old - appeared from around the corner. Accompaning them was fifteen-year-old Lisa Wondermore. They were so astonished at what they saw, they stopped dead in their tracks, turned around and hurried home, where they called all

their girl friends and described the vulgar incident
in embarrassing detail.
Fortunately for Bernie
and Alex, the older boys
didn't learn about it until
Monday when they got to
school.

As Mrs. Patterson tried to
subdue the silliness of her
sons, the family's cat, Princess, emerged from the
house and onto the porch.
My goodness, she said to
herself, *there certainly are a
lot of people in my yard.* She
strolled down the steps to
see what all the commotion was about.

Weezer's waiting had finally paid off; one glimpse of Princess
and he was after her like a streak. Around and around the yard
they ran, which inspired Richard and Robert, the underwear
still on their heads, to race around behind them, with Clark,
Brian and Larry, now also wearing underwear on their heads,
running behind them.

Bernie and Alex made themselves comfortable at the picnic
table and laughed at the parade of animals and boys running
through the yard. They were pretty sure they'd never be invited
to another of the Patterson's parties, and more than likely their
Blazing Bandit days were a thing of the past. With that in
mind, they helped themselves to the two remaining pieces of

chocolate cake. They couldn't wait to describe the underwear incident to Joey Wondermore, who had taken a dislike to the club, even though Clark Olsen had asked him to join about a hundred times. For Bernie and Alex, having Joey for a friend was a lot better than being a Blazing Bandit anyway.

Knowing they'd have to run home as soon as the other boys noticed the cake was gone, Bernie and Alex ate quickly, laughing at the sight of all the older boys, running around the yard with underwear over their heads. Even though they would soon be chased out of the yard, and even though their Blazing Bandit days were over forever, they both decided that all in all, it had actually been a pretty good day.

AUTHOR

Sharon Bushell

Born and raised in Port Angeles, Washington, Sharon Bushell moved to Alaska in 1977. A features writer and columnist for the Anchorage Daily News for many years, Bushell has received numerous awards for her writing, including the Pacific Northwest Excellence in Journalism Award. In 2003 she was honored with the Alaska Governor's Award for the Arts and Humanities for compiling and editing first-person accounts of hundreds of Alaskan old-timers.

In tandem with writing for adults, Bushell has written a series of children's stories whose characters are set in the 1950s. Produced with music and sound effects for local public radio station KBBI, the Bernie stories have aired in public radio stations around the country. They are now in book form as well as CDs.

Bushell's dream for the Bernie stories is quite specific: for children, parents and grandparents to enjoy them together, to discuss their meaning, and to share their own stories with each other, preferably while sitting close and sipping cocoa.

ILLUSTRATOR

Katie Miller

Katie Miller was born in Homer, Alaska on November 10th, 1990. She is an artist, musician, and active sports enthusiast. Miller is looking forward to pursuing these interests as a high school freshman this 2005-2006 school year.

<u>Bernie Jones and the Blazing Bandits</u> is Miller's second book project as an illustrator. Her inspiration comes from many places. Her home is situated in a beautiful location, her life is filled with activities, and she has many friends.

One of her teachers describes Miller as happy, hard working and not willing to settle for anything but the best.